Legend: The Ripper's Eternal Echo

An Immortal Investigator Mystery

Koo Yu

Published by Grey Brume Press
First Paperback Edition: April 2026
Paperback ISBN: 979-8-9955161-0-1

Printed in the United States of America.

To the dreamers who find light even in the fog.

Chapter One

Finn Parker often thought of herself as an ordinary person who had simply wandered too long through the world. Four thousand years, to be precise.

She lived in the modern city of Nordholm now, moving quietly through the city's days. In reality, her metabolism had been frozen in time since 2600 BC, when she was already nearing thirty-four years old. She did not experience aging, sickness, or death. She had lived through the rise and fall of five hundred human lifespans without the distractions of a normal life.

She possessed the wisdom of four millennia and a mastery of martial arts that modern people considered folklore. She still enjoyed the sensation of scaling rooftops and leaping from one lamppost to another. She knew that she could shatter a brick wall with a single, precise gesture. In the ancient past, internal energy and lightness skills were common disciplines. By the eighteenth century, they had become myths. To Finn, they were simply her nature.

Her only companion in this long fate was a man named Wayne. They had been bound to eternity by a choice made in the distant past. They rarely met, choosing instead to exchange new identities and news every thirty years. It was a ritual of remembrance in a world that always forgot them.

Finn was a recluse who hid in the busiest places. She understood the cycles of humanity, the patterns of greed, manipulation, and violence that repeated in every century. Her longevity allowed her to see the truth behind the events that others called history.

One of those cycles occurred in London, 1888.

Finn sat in her study and closed her eyes. The modern sounds of Nordholm faded. In her mind, the fog of the past began to roll in. A vision flickered through her thoughts. She saw a man in a dark wool overcoat, his shirt crisp beneath a high collar, and a wide cravat tied at his chest. His polished boots caught the faint shimmer of fog. From the riverbank, he fell into the freezing water. Gaslight stretched long through the mist, outlining a solitary, resolute figure before the swirling current swallowed him whole.

It was not an illusion, but a memory.

The story did not begin in the present. It began in the shadows of the nineteenth century, where a city's terror was just the opening move.

***

November 1888

Every headline in London shouted the same name, Jack the Ripper had returned.

Yet Finn was in a Mayfair studio, studying oil painting under an instructor from the Royal Academy of Arts. The light was gentle, the model silent in her pose, and the students worked in still concentration, layering color and texture across the canvases. Coal burned quietly in the hearth. The air smelled faintly of oil and plaster. From outside came the rhythm of hooves and carriage wheels on cobblestones.

Life in Mayfair was peaceful and proper. Her maid attended faithfully to her attire and coiffure, ensuring she appeared graceful at every gathering. For Finn, this was only a brief pause in a span of time far longer than anyone could imagine. Her friends, ladies of wealth, cared more about who had danced with whom or which department store had released a new ribbon. The murders in the East End were distant, unpleasant gossip.

During the studio's break, Finn and the others chatted with the model, Annette, who had long posed for artists and was well known to them. When one student, David, remembered she lived in Whitechapel, he asked lightly, "Do you still dare to go out at night?"

Annette stiffened, her voice low. "We hardly go out even in daylight. It's frightening. If your carriage hadn't come for me, I wouldn't have dared come here at all."

"Why?" another naïve student asked.

David sighed. "You haven't heard? Jack the Ripper."

He began to recount the reports, the name, the victims, the horror of their deaths. Faces around the room paled. Some made nervous jokes to ease Annette's fear.

It was the first time Finn had heard the name spoken aloud. In that glittering, perfumed world, the tale felt almost unreal.

***

That evening she returned to her Mayfair apartment.

The parlor was spacious, the fire alive in the grate. White panels with carved borders glowed beneath the light of silver candelabras. Heavy curtains shut out the streetlamps, and shelves lined the walls, filled with art volumes and travel journals. Velvet cushions softened the sofas; the candlelight shimmered across the room, calm and warm.

Emily sat nearby, reading a book of verse. When she looked up, her tone carried its usual gentle humor. "Was the studio pleasant today? And tomorrow, shall we visit Lady Mary? She sent a special invitation."

Finn smiled faintly. "Perhaps."

Emily was the landlord's granddaughter. Orphaned young after her parents met with an accident while traveling, she had lived with her grandparents ever since. Her younger brother remained in their care, still attending school.

When Finn's solicitor arranged the lease, the owners hesitated upon learning that the tenant was an unmarried woman. Only after he offered to pay a higher rent, three years in advance, and guaranteed her respectability as the daughter of a long-standing client did they consent. Still, they worried about propriety, and so Emily was asked to live with her "as a companion." It gave the girl occupation and lent Finn social respectability.

The family held considerable property in London. Through Emily, Finn had met many of the city's notables. The girl was studying at a ladies' college and loved poetry and art; they had grown close quickly.

Finn's maid, Jessica, had already prepared tea and a nightgown before quietly retreating. She was now kneeling by the hearth, arranging firewood, the glow touching her young but cautious face. None of them knew what stayed in her mind, the image of Annette's frightened eyes, and the murders that stained the news.

That season's fog was heavier than usual, pressing over the city as if it meant to swallow it whole. Between the suffocating routine and the reports of women killed in the streets, a restlessness began to stir within her. Emily, unaware, continued to chatter about which classmate had bought a new gown.

Finn decided to return to an old habit, investigation. Perhaps she could learn more about this killer.

Seated alone on the sofa, she thought, *Where should I begin?*

Annette came to mind. Since she lived in Whitechapel, she might know something others overlooked. Finn would not see her again until the next class, but tomorrow she could visit the library first, to read about this "Ripper." Then another thought followed, Emily's uncle, Paul Ashworth, was a journalist. Through him, she might hear the truth.

Finn glanced at Emily, still absorbed in her poetry. "Emily," she said casually, "you mentioned that your uncle Paul is a reporter, didn't you? Would you ask if he might join us for lunch? There are a few things I'd like to ask him."

Emily did not question why. Her eyes glinted with amusement, and she nodded. She had long grown used to Finn's peculiarities, her disinterest in social gossip, her long hours with books not all considered proper reading for a lady. Both Emily and Jessica had learned to accept it. They were, in their way, her most loyal companions.

The next morning, Finn declined Emily's invitation for a walk. After reminding her to arrange the luncheon, she set out alone for the library.

It was a respected public reading room in London's West End. Pale daylight filtered through arched windows. Gas lamps glowed against the fog-stained walls, their light dim and flickering.

The hall was hushed but not empty. Rows of wooden tables stretched beneath the high ceiling. The air smelled of paper and coal smoke. Men murmured over the latest editions, pages rustled, pens scratched faintly across paper. From one corner came a low voice, "Another one." Others grumbled about the editors' exaggerations.

Finn walked to the newspaper stand and took *The Times* and *The Star*.

The headline read,

"Another Whitechapel Murder, After a Month of Silence, Jack the Ripper Strikes Again."

The Times was restrained, listing the victim's name, age, and manner of death with grim precision, followed by details of earlier cases.

The Star was fevered, almost gleeful,

"The killer moves through the fog like a phantom, his blade flashing with madness, turning the East End into hell itself!"

The newest victim had died the previous night. The article compared her to the others, Nichols, Chapman, Stride, Eddowes. All were prostitutes, throats cut, bodies mutilated. But Kelly, only twenty-five, had been killed in her own room, her body dismembered beyond recognition.

Finn's fingertips brushed ink across the page before she realized she had stopped breathing. Kelly had not died in the street.

In the records room she asked an attendant to bring bound newspaper volumes. He handed her a heavy leather tome, warning, "Careful, the paper is fragile."

She sat and opened the yellowed pages, noting key details in her notebook. Soon she saw how accounts contradicted one another. *A thin, unkempt man with tangled hair. A tall, well-dressed gentleman seen nearby. An immigrant.* Each report carried its own prejudice.

This was no mere confusion. It was a web of contradictions, deliberately woven to blur the truth.

Closing the notebook, she knew she could no longer rely on the papers.

As she returned the volume, two men whispered nearby, "They say the police got a letter from the killer, with blood on it. No one knows if it's real."

Finn listened without turning. If it was true, then the murderer wanted more than death, he wanted to manipulate fear itself. These reports, she thought, were part of the fog he had made, concealing his real shadow within it.

***

When Finn came home, Emily was already dressed and waiting in the parlor, a folded letter in her hand and a mischievous spark in her eyes.

"I've arranged it," she said. "Lunch at the Crown." A blush rose on her cheeks. "Uncle Paul asked why I wanted to meet, so I told him I needed advice about women's employment."

Finn laughed softly. "Am I the one seeking work, then?"

Emily made a playful face. "Of course not. Grandfather always said our tenant is comfortably wealthy. I'll just claim I'm considering a career."

Her tone was teasing, but Finn felt a quiet warmth. She reached out, briefly drew the girl into an affectionate half-embrace, and murmured, "Thank you."

After a pause she added honestly, "Yesterday at the studio they spoke about the Whitechapel murders. The killer has even been given a name, Jack the Ripper. Since Annette lives there, I'd like to know more."

Emily's expression grew serious. "Then you went to the library today, to read about it?"

Finn nodded. Her perceptiveness never failed to impress.

Emily thought for a moment, then smiled suddenly. "I know how to tell Uncle Paul. If you mention you're interested in the murders, it might sound odd. But he already knows I'm curious about journalism. I'll say I want to learn how reporters follow such a story, and you're joining me as a friend for advice. That will sound perfectly natural."

Finn couldn't help but smile. "You've planned it well."

Emily lifted her chin with mock pride, looking like a small general pleased with her strategy.

A carriage stopped outside. Emily and Finn climbed in together, the hooves ringing briskly against the stones as they rode toward the Crown in the West End.

The restaurant stood near Fleet Street, close to the offices of newspapers and law firms, a place favored by reporters and barristers. Inside, the noon rush had begun, waiters in white shirts and black vests moved between tables with trays of meat pies, beer, and steaming lamb stew. The air was thick with talk, tobacco, and the rustle of newspapers.

Paul was already waiting by the window. Around forty, with slightly disordered dark brown hair and a black coat worn at the edges, he kept a notebook open beside him as if unwilling to part from it even at meals. He rose when they entered, serious yet kind, his expression softening when he looked at Emily.

"Finn, this is my uncle, Paul," Emily said.

"We met briefly in the street last month," Finn said, offering her hand. "It's a pleasure to meet properly."

His grip was firm, the palm roughened by years of writing. "You're quite well-known in our family," he said with a wry smile.

He came from a distinguished family and was respected within the profession. He had chosen journalism over comfort, building his career through quiet persistence rather than privilege. The independence and defiance showed in his tired but steady eyes.

Turning back to Emily, he asked, "So you want to talk about women's employment?"

Emily blinked playfully but answered with composure. "Yes, Uncle. I've always been curious about the newspaper world, but I don't know if women can truly find a place there. I'd like your advice."

Paul's lips curved with quiet amusement. He did not expose her pretext. Instead, he gestured for them to sit.

A waiter brought beer and menus. Once their orders were placed, Paul thumbed through his notebook and spoke in a low tone. "If you want to understand how a reporter hunts for stories, the most difficult one right now is the Whitechapel murders."

Emily feigned surprise and glanced at Finn, eyes bright with confirmation. "That case fascinates me," she said. "How would a reporter even begin?"

Paul adjusted his spectacles, his tone turning grave. "We're always in a tug-of-war with the police. They want to keep the panic down, while we must print the truth, however ugly. The city's already terrified. Some papers have even received letters from someone claiming to be the killer. He signed them *Jack the Ripper.*"

Finn spoke quietly. "Those letters are real?"

Paul's gaze sharpened. "One of them came with a piece of kidney. The police denied it, but I've seen the report myself. Whether it's genuine or not, it shows that the killer wants more than blood. He wants control, over the city's fear."

Finn drew a slow breath. The contradictions she had noted in the papers now made sense. Someone was weaving the confusion deliberately.

Emily asked lightly, "And if a reporter were to pursue the story, how would they do it?"

Paul's eyes lingered on her. "You start with sources. Printed news is never enough. You need to speak to officers, witnesses, even the victims' acquaintances, anyone close to the truth."

He took a drink, weariness flickering behind his gaze. "But the police despise reporters, especially in this case. They're afraid of exposure. They'll tell us as little as they can."

Finn said softly, "Then you rely on…informants?"

A thin smile crossed his face. "Exactly. If you're lucky, you find a constable willing to talk. Luckier still, a street informant. They'll sell you anything for a coin."

Emily nodded thoughtfully, then asked in an innocent tone, "And have you met such people?"

Paul closed his notebook, fingers tapping its cover. "There's one man, O'Leary. Irish, fond of drink, half his stories worthless, but sometimes he knows things no one else does. He said he saw a well-dressed gentleman near Dorset Street the night before the last murder."

Finn felt a faint tremor of recognition. The detail matched what she had noticed in the conflicting accounts.

Paul leaned back slightly, half-smiling. "If you truly wish to chase this story, find O'Leary. He works the Spitalfields Market by day, hauling goods, and spends his evenings drunk in the taverns nearby."

The waiter returned with their meals, breaking the tension. Knives and forks clinked softly. Emily kept her composure, but Finn saw the glance she stole toward her, knowing exactly what she was thinking.

"Do all reporters have their own informants?" Emily asked.

Paul shook his head. "If only. Most informants talk to whoever pays or protects them. This trade runs on risk and nerve. Sometimes buying a drunk a pint earns you a fragment of truth."

His gaze drifted to the window, the lamplight catching the fatigue in his face. "But there are no true friends on the streets. Every smile can turn into a knife. Whitechapel is no exception."

Emily swallowed. "It sounds even more dangerous than I imagined."

Finn glanced at her but said nothing.

Paul turned back, his voice lighter. "So, do you still want to be a reporter? You might begin as a contributor, perhaps write a few trial pieces."

Emily laughed softly. "Let me think about it."

He smiled, though his final words were edged with warning. "Even for a man, walking those streets alone is risky. Remember this, news is not poetry. It drags people into the mud, not the garden. For women, that danger is doubled."

When lunch ended, they stepped out into the wind. The cold slipped down their collars. Emily shivered, then looked at Finn and asked quietly, "Will you go find that man?"

Finn did not answer. She simply took Emily's hand, and together they walked toward the waiting carriage.

Chapter Two

The next day Finn attended the class as usual, though this time with another purpose in mind.

After the session, she found a pretext to keep Annette back and told her she was writing a book on "the cultures of London's districts," asking if Annette would guide her through the East End. Annette refused at once. Because of the Ripper, she said, she did not even dare go out by day. Finn had expected the refusal, so she proposed another plan. She would lodge at Annette's rooms, and she had already booked Annette a few nights at the Brown Hotel, even bought her several dresses suitable for a lady of fashion so she could blend in naturally at the hotel.

Finn liked Annette very much. She was sweet and quick, only born to hard fortune, without a proper education, making her living by her looks. Among working-class women her situation was not uncommon. What choices did women have then. Finn truly hoped Annette could rise beyond her birth and have a better future.

Back home, Finn told Emily and Jessica she would be away for a few days. Emily only widened her eyes at her, said nothing more. Jessica packed clothes and necessities and saw

Finn to the carriage. As Finn left, Emily only said softly, "Be careful."

The carriage set her down on Hanbury Street. The road was narrow and crowded, flanked by gray rows of houses. Annette's home was on the first floor of an old building above a butcher's shop. The air carried a mix of iron and damp mold.

Annette was waiting below. She led Finn through the rooms, and because the place was small the introduction ended quickly.

"Do you want me to take you around?" she asked, a little hesitant.

"No need. I brought a map," Finn said, pointing to her satchel.

Annette sank into a chair with relief.

"Are you truly this afraid?" Finn asked carefully.

"Yes," Anne said, lowering her voice. "I heard they all had their throats cut, and the killer even took their organs." She spoke very softly, as if afraid the Ripper was listening in the dark.

"Did you know the victims?" Finn pressed. "The police and the papers call them prostitutes, but I know they only want to label the case that way to ease public fear."

Annette nodded. "I knew them. They lived near me. They were not the shameless sort people imagine. They were only trying to live."

Finn watched her. Annette drew a long breath, as if steeling herself.

"Do you want to hear their stories?"

Finn nodded. "Only if it will not hurt you too much. I want to record what truly happened."

"Perhaps saying it will help," Annette whispered. "I live in fear, always thinking I could end the same way. The second killing happened just behind this street. I often wonder if I ever crossed paths with him. Even when I stay indoors, I fear ending like Mary Jane Kelly, murdered in her own room."

She broke down. Finn patted her shoulder lightly. After a while she raised her head, voice hoarse.

"Forgive me. Let me speak slowly. The carriage comes in half an hour. I am grateful you are letting me leave for a while."

She wiped her tears and began.

Those women were not what people imagined. Some were mothers, some widows, some beaten and driven back to the street. Most lived by washing, mending, cleaning, seeking a little coin, a little shelter.

The last of them, Mary Jane Kelly, was the youngest and most heartbreaking. Pretty and spirited, she had known better days, but life narrowed around her until she died alone in her dark Whitechapel room. Anne's voice sank lower with each name. Only the hiss of the gas lamp filled the silence, its flame trembling in her tear-bright eyes.

When she finished, the room grew so still they could hear each other breathe.

Head bowed, her tone calm but trembling, she had actually known Mary Jane Kelly. A month earlier, she, Kelly,

and a friend had attended a private dinner given by a gentleman of rank. Kelly had been lively and radiant that night.
Halfway through the recollection, Anne's tears fell again.

Finn took her hand and let her rest. She had already arranged for the Brown Hotel to cover her stay and meals, and
she slipped some pocket money into her hand. Annette
thanked her in a whisper, nodding again and again.

As night deepened and she changed into the clothes
Finn had brought, Finn asked quietly about the private dinner.
When the carriage arrived, she saw Annette out, giving the
coachman a generous gratuity and firm instruction to treat
her as a lady of respect.

Left alone, Finn returned to the window and matched
what lay before her to the lines on her map. Spitalfields Market was only a few streets away. On the map she circled the
murder sites from the past two months. The black marks sat
on her mind like a brand. Perhaps tomorrow she should walk
them herself.

***

Paul had mentioned O'Leary, a short, thickset drunk with a
bristling beard and a battered deerstalker. Finn glanced out at
the street. Men like that seemed to be everywhere here.

Before dusk she changed at Annette's rooms into the
maid's clothes she had prepared, then walked toward Spitalfields Market to try her luck. The day's crowd had already
thinned. Only scattered workers and idlers remained. She

noticed a few children playing at a corner and took out a shilling, letting it glint before their eyes.

"Have you seen an Irishman who drinks, short and stocky, full beard, always in a ragged deerstalker?" she asked in a low voice.

The children looked at one another. One raised a hand and pointed to a man smoking by a side door. "Do not know his name, but the grown-ups call him the Irishman."

Finn looked up. The description fit. She gave the boy the shilling, took out another, and said softly, "Count to five, then shout 'O'Leary' and see if he reacts."

The boy's eyes lit. He took the coin and did as told. At the cry of "O'Leary!" the short man snapped his head around and swore, "Off with you, brats!" The children burst into laughter and scattered.

In that instant Finn was sure who he was.

After dark she slipped into the fog-filled market. Gaslight flickered. Tavern noise drifted from afar. She checked several public houses and at last saw O'Leary at the bar of a small one at the far end of the market.

She studied the surroundings, chose a dim gallery on the second floor of the market opposite, vaulted up with practiced ease, and settled into the shadow where the lamplight could not reach.

A little over an hour later, O'Leary appeared sooner than she expected, humming off-key and walking with careless cheer.

She followed along the eaves. He turned into a narrow street, entered a dilapidated building, and climbed the stairs.

Finn waited, then dropped lightly, crossed to the opposite landing, and held her breath to listen. The breath inside was wrong. Not heavy. Controlled. Deliberately quiet. Not the easy rhythm of a man at rest.

Her nerves tightened. She took out a metal strip with a toothed end, teased the lock twice, and the door yielded at once. The room was dark. As her eyes adjusted, a rush of air grazed her ear. She twisted aside. A short blade flashed in the dark.

She caught the attacker's wrist. He cried out. She drew back to drive her elbow into his chest, and in the edge of her sight saw O'Leary sprawled on the floor, blood surging from his neck.

She released the attacker's wrist and slipped to O'Leary's side. Her fingers found the points beneath his earlobe and along the jaw, pressing to slow the blood while she kept alert for a second strike. The flow eased. She lifted his head carefully, touched two points at the nape and spine, then set it down again.

When she turned to search for the knifeman, only O'Leary's shallow breaths remained. The room was silent.

She moved inward. A window stood wide, large enough for a man to pass. She leaned out. Night had fallen. The fog closed the view. She swept out along the window line, hoping for a glimpse of him. After a circuit there was no trace. There were too many levels and corners to hide in. With O'Leary's condition weighing on her, she returned to him, fixed her mind on him again, bound the wound with a strip torn from his shirt, pressed points again to slow the blood, then lifted him and ran for the stairs.

The street was strangely quiet. She recalled the way to Annette's Hanbury Street, traced it to the hospital marked on her map, and headed straight for the London Hospital on Whitechapel Road. As she moved, she steadied her breathing and pressed her palms to his chest, channeling her strength through steady rhythm, willing her own pulse to guide his.

At the entrance she set him down and shouted for help. When she saw the physicians rush out, she turned and slipped back into the fog.

She returned to O'Leary's rooms to look for traces of the attacker. The place was a chaos of junk and broken furniture, the air stale with old wood and drink. Men like him were common here. Who would risk killing a poor man known for the bottle? The only reason was that he had seen something vital and had to be silenced. Yet if so, the attack might make others believe him more, not less. Or perhaps someone wanted the world to believe him, and therefore wanted him quiet.

She searched the table and drawers. Beside an old wooden chest stood two battered cartons filled with odds and ends, children's clothes, yellowed papers, broken toys. The papers bore the name Helen Jones. In the chest she found a few faded photographs, a young O'Leary with a woman and a boy, not yet grown. On the back of one was a scrawl, Sarah

& Richard. His family, perhaps. Beneath them lay several letters in an unpracticed hand, signed only M, and a neatly folded set of children's clothes.

She paused, then went to the left-hand window to see if the knifeman had left any trace.

The scene from moments before rose before her eyes, O'Leary on the floor, her fingers closing points to staunch the blood, lifting his head, all in an instant. When she returned to the left window, the attacker was gone. Unless he, too, had skills to run the roofs, he could not have vanished so cleanly. Finn set that aside and considered where he might have lain in wait.

She stepped out, moved four or five paces along the awning toward the inner street, and found it. In a recess lay scuffed dust and black grit. He had hidden there last night.

Which meant he knew the area perfectly. To be safe she wrapped some of the dust and grit in her handkerchief.

She left the rooms. It was a little past four. Wheels and calls were sounding already. Men pushed barrows toward the market. A few maids hurried by with baskets to prepare breakfasts. In her maid's clothes she drew no notice at all.

Circling back to the building, she found neighbors already talking. They said O'Leary had been stabbed the night before and was at death's door, found for some reason at the London Hospital. Some guessed he had crawled there himself. Finn let a thought form and casually spread the tale that a tall man had carried him.

She spoke with several old neighbors deep in discussion. Some mentioned his past. After his wife and child died, he left his home for London. He had once been close to a mother and boy who lived next door. He had doted on the child. When the mother died, the boy went missing. O'Leary searched for months without success and drowned himself further in drink.

Finn noted the gossip and walked toward the public house. Several policemen were questioning people about O'Leary's movements the previous night.

The barman was crouched at the door, resigned, a knot of people talking all at once around him. He looked up and saw her, kept his face heavy, and drew on his cigarette.

She went close and kept her voice low. "What are the police after."

He looked her over. "Move along, foolish girl. Do not meddle."

Finn took two pounds from her pocket and let them turn between her fingers. "A reporter just slipped me five pounds," she said quietly, "told me to ask about O'Leary. Give me a little, and these two are yours."

His eyes lit. He held out his hand. "Money first."

She stepped back half a pace, smiling. "Say something and we will see. Afraid I'll run?"

He rubbed his chin and snorted. "If you know that Irishman was stabbed, why ask what the police want."

"Perhaps they want something else," Finn said mildly.

He looked at her, then spoke. "I was closing when a few officers burst in, asking about the Irishman. I told them he left early."

"Early?" Finn asked.

He nodded. "Aye. He stays till two most nights. Yesterday he had one drink, left after nine. Not his way."

Finn considered, then lowered her voice. "What else is worth two pounds? I do not hand out money for nothing." She smiled. "Some say he was attacked because he saw the Ripper's face. What do you think?"

The barman curled his lip. "He bragged he had, and that he got ten pounds for it."

"Do you believe him?" Finn asked.

"He comes late on Wednesdays. Has to deliver fresh goods to a restaurant on Dorset Street first." He paused, weighing it, then dropped his voice. "Maybe he did see something."

He thought again before adding, "A few nights ago he was blind drunk. Someone teased him, and he blurted he had seen not only a well-dressed gentleman on Dorset Street, he had seen a man walking with that gentleman."

"Who was the man," Finn asked at once.

"Do not know. Some tried to press him then, but he shut up. Next day when they asked again, he said he was drunk and talking nonsense."

He took another drag, then added, "Last night he drank alone. Spoke to no one. Finished and left."

Finn studied him. He did not seem to be lying, though he had kept something back. She laid the two pounds in his palm.

He grinned and pocketed them. "I may have heard something about the attack, or about the Ripper." he said. "Would your reporter friend pay more, say ten pounds?"

Finn feigned hesitation, then said, "If it proves of true importance, ten pounds will be easily found. I will come again at dusk tomorrow."

To search further, she went to the places where the victims had died. Every corner had its witness, a shadow, a cry, a stranger hurrying away. The stories were fragments, waiting to be joined.

She walked the wet streets of Whitechapel, tracing the last paths of the five women. At Buck's Row, where Mary Ann Nichols fell, the stones still seemed to breathe. A neighbor whispered, "There was no cry. The throat was cut at once." The gaslight barely touched the fog; the street felt sealed in silence.

Hanbury Street, Berner Street, Mitre Square, each corner whispered the same story in a different voice, a startled cry, a fence marked by struggle, a wall that remembered a shadow. The pattern was clear enough; the killer struck and vanished before the city even stirred.

Then Dorset Street. Mary Jane Kelly had died indoors. A narrow door, a shabby window, they had kept nothing out. A room is crueller than a corner, no passersby, no gaslight, only a bed that turns into a stage. Finn examined the frame and latch. No sign of force. Kelly must have opened the door herself, cautious but not to him. Someone she knew. Someone trusted. Before dawn, the door opened and death stepped in.

When Finn had walked all five final places, she returned to Annette's to rest. She spread out her notes. Patterns began to surface. Only Kelly worked indoors. All were single. All died in the city's dead hours, between night and morning, when fog pressed down and even London seemed to hold its breath. The fog gave the killer his perfect screen, to appear and vanish without a sound.

She drew a heavy circle around the entry "private dinner." It might not be tied directly to the Ripper, yet the gathering itself was intriguing.

She closed her notebook, letting the pieces settle in her mind.

At dusk she returned to the public house. Fog rose along the corner. Gaslight sank into the gray. The street looked unnaturally still. Inside the air was stale. She had expected the same barman, but a stranger stood polishing glasses behind the counter.

He looked up. His voice was hoarse and low, as if hiding his fatigue. The barman had not returned. Someone had knocked at his door with no answer. Tonight the place was left to this one man.

Unease moved quietly through Finn. The barman had seemed to be holding something back. His disappearance looked like proof of it. She asked for the address, wrote it down quickly, and turned to go.

The mist thickened. She hurried along the stones until the wooden door came into view. She breathed once and prayed she would not find blood and shadow tangled again. Inside was oddly quiet. No footsteps. No stench. She slipped the latch with a tool and entered.

No one. A few yellowed pages lay on the table with names of Dublin neighbors. An old work cap hung by the wall, showing he had once labored in Ireland. From such details Finn was nearly certain his tie with O'Leary ran deeper than most knew.

She went out the window again and returned to the tavern, then drew the man into casual talk. In a few lines he admitted it. They were old friends. The weight in Finn's chest settled like lead. The disappearance was not a coincidence.

The streets had emptied. A few lamps burned low as she made her way toward Dorset Street.

She opened the door of the little room. Old blood hit her nose. Stains had seeped into the floorboards. She stepped over them and glanced around at the lone bed and the scattered furniture. This had been the killer's cruellest stage.

She bent to check the bedside table. A few crumpled papers slid from torn cloth. One bore the printed heading "Druitt." The letters were small, clearly from a printed notepaper, not handwritten. It could have been a scrap from a solicitor's office or a shop. The name still struck her, a sudden weight in the chest.

She clipped the sheet into her notebook. Then she saw another with the same heading. She had already, without noticing, used it as scrap. One had been found at Annette's home. One lay now at the murder scene. It might mean nothing at all. Or it might point to a hidden line.

Finn frowned and put the papers away. The most obvious clues often deserved the most doubt. Was "Druitt" only coincidence? or had someone placed it on purpose?

She drew a steady breath, closed her notebook, and, after a final glance toward the window, slipped out, drawing the door softly to.

***

Emily could not put Finn from her mind. The unease clung to her, heavy in her chest. If Finn truly had gone to Whitechapel, then the one who might know was Annette.

In the studio she mentioned needing a carriage, knowing the coachman would likely know the address. When she asked, he smiled and said Annette was staying at the Brown Hotel.

The hotel's marble front gleamed in the sun. Inside, the air smelled of polish and flowers. At the desk, the clerk confirmed Annette was taking tea in the restaurant and led Emily in.

By the window Annette sat in an elegant gown, a stand of cakes before her. Her calmness struck Emily like a rebuke.

Annette looked up in surprise, then smiled and motioned for her to sit. Emily asked at once about Finn. Annette said Finn was lodging at her Hanbury Street rooms. She herself had moved to the hotel and did not know Finn's movements.

Emily's heart sank. Finn was alone in Whitechapel now. The worry in her thickened. She had the coachman take her straight to Hanbury Street. The carriage jolted along gray streets, and by dusk they arrived. The corner was unusually still. No light in the windows. No sound. Finn was out.

Following Annette's earlier hint, Emily found a spare key, opened the door, and went in. The rooms were simple. An empty chair stood by the window. She set down her wrap, lit a lamp, and decided to wait for Finn's return.

Sitting by the window, she drifted into sleep without meaning to. A little knock, as of wood taking weight, woke her. Night had already fallen outside. The silence was unnatural. She rubbed her eyes. Finn was still absent. Worry rose again. She stood and pushed open the shut window, letting the cool air in to clear the close room.

The thought struck her, this was where the Ripper moved. She reached to close the window. At that instant the fog boiled and a shadow flicked. A gloved hand shot in and clamped the frame. The glove's knuckles looked cold under the light.

Emily gasped. Her body locked. The hand forced the sash wider, inch by inch. She tried to cry out, but only a rasp came, shivering around the room. The intruder did not answer. He put more weight on the frame. The window creaked and began to yield.

Emily stumbled back and ran for the door. The lamp's light wavered. Her skirt rasped on the floor, urging her to flee. Just as her fingers were reaching the handle, metal clicked behind her. The knife was out. She turned her head. Steel flashed in the fogged light. Cold went through her. Her step faltered. The blade was about to strike when the man stopped, staring at her face.

That heartbeat of hesitation saved her. By instinct she turned, swept a hand over the table, and seized the oil lamp. She hurled it at the shadow by the window. Glass burst. Flame jumped. Oil sprayed. A grunt sounded, then the flame died. The shadow did not withdraw. He lunged in, his knife glinting. He caught her arm with the same hand that held the blade, pinning her against the table. His other hand clamped her mouth and nose, iron-tight.

Emily struggled. Air would not come. Her chest fought for breath. Darkness crept at the edge of her sight. A roar filled her ears. She tried to push the smothering hand away, but her strength was gone. Panic, fear, and suffocation tangled inside her. Only broken sobs came. Her fingertips clawed at his sleeve. Then his grip shifted. The knife flashed at the edge of her vision, cold enough to steal the air. A black glove brushed her cheek. His breath was close and colder still. Death seemed to be coming.

A sharp rush split the air. He grunted. The hand over her mouth loosened, though the other still gripped her arm. Emily sagged, falling against him.

Finn vaulted through the window. The man saw her and flung Emily hard in her direction. Finn had only a heartbeat to choose. She caught Emily as the man tore the door open and vanished into the hall.

"This time I will not let you run," Finn said between her teeth, her voice low as steel.

Emily slumped to the floor. Finn knelt, patted her cheek twice to check her breathing, then pressed two points between the shoulder and neck. The body slackened; a brief sleep steadied her breath. Finn set her in a safe shadow and rose at once.

Outside, the fog was thicker. Lantern light drowned in the wet. The street wore a gray veil. His back was already thinning to a black line ahead, near the end of Hanbury Street.

Finn adjusted her footing, pushed off the slick stones, and vaulted to the eaves of the second floor. Roof to roof, she crossed in silence, her steps light and sure.

He wove left and right, threading alleys like a rat used to the corners. When he turned into a narrow cut off Brick Lane, she was only a few yards behind. The lamplight stretched across the wet brick. As she pressed on, the lane bent. He slipped into shadow, as if down a seam beneath the bridge.

Finn dropped to the street and reached the bend. He was gone. She checked the ground, fresh wet marks, a kicked-aside crate, the faint scuff of a heel, but found nothing. The fog muffled every sound. The lane was still enough to turn thought inward.

She cursed under her breath but did not linger. Emily still needed her. The pressure point would hold only for a while. Real recovery would show when the girl woke. Finn steadied her breath and turned back. She would bring back what she had found. Any lapse, and the truth would vanish again.

***

Finn returned to find Emily still asleep. She pressed lightly at the point and released it.

Emily stirred, her lashes trembling like someone rising from deep water. She started awake and seized Finn's arm.

"He almost strangled me," she said hoarsely.

Finn helped her to sit and gave her water.

"Did he mean to kill me. Was it my fault for opening the window," Emily asked.

Finn asked for the details. Emily said that once she opened the window the man was inside almost at once. Finn was sure the target had been whoever was in the rooms.

"Why did he let go," Emily asked, still shaking. "Were you not afraid? Thank goodness you came back."

Finn only said perhaps the noise had startled him. Emily was too shaken. Finn would not press her. She herself had seen only a shape. The table lamp had fallen and gone out. The room was black. Only the weak street gaslight gave her a glimpse. A scarf covered his face. He was tall and slim, moved with speed, probably young.

Finn soothed her and called her brave for walking into Whitechapel alone. Emily insisted on staying with her. There was no retreat in her eyes, only resolve. The simple courage warmed Finn. She nodded and agreed to share what she learned.

Finn laid out what they had so far. Letters bearing the name Druitt had appeared both at Annette's and in Kelly's room. The private dinners were the only shared ground between them.

The next morning they went to the Brown Hotel to meet Annette. She was seated in a corner of the lobby, a cloak about her shoulders. When she saw Finn and Emily, her face brightened.

"I am much obliged to you for the arrangements," she said. "The room is most comfortable."

"It was no trouble," Finn replied. "There are a few names we wished to ask you about. In particular, Druitt."

Annette's expression seemed to stiffen for a glance. She lowered her voice. "He was once my public defender."

Seeing they did not speak, she added, "Sometimes he found me work."

"What kind of work," Emily asked.

"Anything," Annette said, fingers worrying the edge of her cloak and avoiding their eyes. "Drinking, dinners, watching a place. Sometimes he introduced us to clients."

"You mentioned you met Kelly at an official's party. Was that arranged by him," Finn asked.

She shook her head, then corrected herself. "Yes. He would send a carriage to take us to wherever the client wanted. The official was an old client of mine."

"And that night, besides Kelly, who else," Finn asked.

"There was a woman called Ashley," Annette said, frowning. "I did not know her. Only that she and Kelly were neighbors, somewhere around Dorset Street."

"Do you remember the address. And the official's name," Finn asked.

"In Belgravia. I do not know the exact place. I do not know the official's name either. We only called him 'Sir.' He was bald, tall, with a large belly." Annette looked embarrassed but could not help smiling. "I hope that helps."

They thanked her and extended her stay by a week. Home was not safe.

Finn and Emily divided the work. Finn asked Emily to find Paul and have him check recent records of young women's deaths. Finn had a bad feeling. They agreed to return to the Mayfair house that night and not remain at Annette's.

Finn followed the line to Dorset Street. The grocer at the corner pointed across, saying that Ashley had shared a room with others and had not been back for over a month. Finn knocked. A woman with a hard face opened.

"I am her sister," Finn said. "I know she has not returned. May I look at her room."

"It has been let," the woman said coldly. "If you want her things, I can sell them to you."

Finn took a pound from her pocket. The woman said at once, "They are in the kitchen."

In a carton Finn found only a few belongings. The clothes had likely been pawned; only scraps remained. Among them lay a pre-printed letterhead bearing the name Druitt. The sight of it made her heart sink. The name itself felt like a thorn buried deep, impossible to draw out.

Night drew on. Finn returned to the Mayfair house and laid the clues out again and again. Soon Emily came back and said she had arranged to see Paul at noon the next day.

Chapter Three

At noon the next day they met in a small tavern near Fleet Street. Paul had dark crescents under his eyes and looked exhausted, though he still wore his reporter's waistcoat, neat as ever. He set a stack of papers on the table and fixed his gaze on them.

"The information you wanted… you are not investigating the Ripper, are you?" His tone was harsh.

"We are only doing some research. It should not be dangerous, should it. We are not going to Whitechapel," Emily said, prepared with her answer.

"You had better not go to Whitechapel. If you do, you may be the next victims." Paul's voice stayed sharp, but he turned to Finn. "You are not going to fool around with her, are you."

"No. I am writing a book on the cultures of London's districts. I happened to hear of Whitechapel and want to write about the hardship of the new immigrants there, with a little on the Ripper for context. Emily is helping me gather information." Finn presented the same pretext again.

Paul was half convinced. He spoke more gently. "Do you know the O'Leary I mentioned the other day. He had his throat cut in the street. Even so, he was saved, but he is still unconscious. If a grown man can come to grief, you must not think of going after the Ripper."

"Does that mean the man he saw is very likely the Ripper," Finn asked.

"Yesterday the police questioned the colleague who bought that tip from O'Leary. I believe they are very interested in that well-dressed gentleman on Dorset Street."

Finn nodded.

"Assaults in Whitechapel are not limited to O'Leary. Do not set foot there," Paul repeated, tireless in warning them.

After a while he picked up his notebook. "Here is what I found in the newspaper records. Women who have died on London's streets in the past six months." He scratched his chin and went on. "I have marked the discovery sites on this map. Whitechapel accounts for nine tenths."

"These are the related reports, with descriptions of appearance, ages, and the times they went missing." He drew out a sheaf of papers for Finn.

"I am ashamed. Many bodies in Whitechapel end as headless cases with no resolution. In other districts the rate of solving is higher." Finn saw the fatigue and anger in his eyes. In that moment Paul was no longer only a reporter. He looked like a lone knight carrying the truth. His voice shook with feeling, but his hand pressed the glass steadily, refusing to show weakness.

"As for the missing person reports, they are here as well. Nothing unusual. Some return home after a few days. Some families receive letters saying they are safe after a time."

"You asked me to find a powerful man living in Belgravia. Everyone in Belgravia is powerful, but fitting your description, bald, tall, and fat, I believe there is only one. A figure with good reach in the Home Office system, named Sir Reginald Whitmore."

Finn turned the name over in her mind and lifted her eyes for Paul to continue.

He drew out his last page and tapped it with a knuckle. "Sir Reginald Whitmore. His title is adviser at the undersecretary level in the Home Office system. He does not attend Parliament often, but is long present in departmental meetings. His house in Belgravia is near Eaton Place. The back lane is a stable mews. The coachmen call it Eaton Mews."

Finn nodded and fixed the address in her memory. The next step was to see whether this western alley joined the same line as the eastern blood cases.

Emily asked in a low voice, "What about his reputation."

His public image is that of a philanthropist. He funds veterans' charities and poor districts, and with several members of Parliament he has done much for Whitechapel parish. He is well connected in politics and sometimes writes on public order."

Paul's voice dropped a shade lower. "In private, though, he keeps close ties with certain arms suppliers and is a regular at a gentlemen's club in St James's. According to one of the waiters there, Whitmore enjoys a cigar and brandy after dinner, leaves around ten, and reaches home near midnight."

Finn added, "What of his household."

"Her ladyship is often taking the waters in Bath or gone to visit family. The house is run mainly by an older butler and a young assistant in Sir Reginald's employ. I hear that when there are special engagements the servants are given leave, except for those two," Paul said, turning a page.

"Why are you looking for this 'philanthropist'. In London, on the list of men you should never offend, Sir Reginald is one of them. Remember that many people have a dark side. Do not stir the hornets' nest."

He pushed the top page toward them. "This is the documentation I just mentioned." He paused and spoke to Emily. "My younger brother is stubborn to a fault, and you have inherited all his virtues and his flaws." He sounded a little wistful. "I know you will not listen to me. But if you change from talk on paper to action in the street, at least inform me and let me go with you."

"As for you, Finn, you have wealth beyond counting, but the world is dangerous. It is not like your bright Mayfair house with only one side to it." He stopped. "In any case, if you do anything, tell me."

He set two shillings on the table, waved a hand, and left.

Finn was not the sheltered heiress he imagined, yet his words touched something in her. He was only a man of letters. If he had faced last night's Ripper head-on, he might not have escaped.

Seeing Finn silent, Emily thought Paul's words had stung her. She spoke softly to comfort her and said her uncle's temper had always been like that, that Finn should not take it to heart.

Finn shook her head and spoke calmly. "Your uncle is a good man. Very gallant." Then she added, "Let us go back, put our materials in order, and see what else we can find."

Back home she and Emily sat at the desk and wrote,

1. Kelly, Ashley, and Annette have a point of contact with Druitt. Their homes contain notepaper printed with Druitt's name.
2. Kelly has been killed, Ashley is missing.
3. The man who attacked Emily, was he the Ripper? Was he intending to kill Annette?
4. Private dinners. Sir Reginald.

Finn thought for a moment. A hypothesis took shape. Ashley had very likely come to harm as well, only in circumstances unlike the other victims. Because the body had not been dismembered, the case had not been classed under the Ripper and so had not appeared in the papers.

She reviewed the files on the table and pointed to the stack, asking Emily to look for any cases like Ashley's. Emily nodded and began to go through them page by page.

Only the sound of paper turning remained in the room. Finn paced by the window, thinking of the next step.

She turned to Emily and asked whether an acquaintance might arrange an introduction to Sir Reginald, using the earlier pretext of interviewing him for a book on London's districts and his views on veterans and Whitechapel. It would draw no suspicion and gain them time.

Emily nodded. "Lady Mary can probably help. Her late husband supported the veterans."

"Excellent." Finn gave her a brief embrace, struck again by how useful Emily's family connections could be.

The next morning the fog had not lifted. Carriage ruts rattled on the paving stones like an uneasy omen. Emily went out to see Lady Mary and arrange the introduction. Finn remained at home and reviewed the notes they had ordered the night before. Druitt's name appeared again and again. It was not only on Annette's and Kelly's notepaper. His hand could be found among the effects Ashley left behind. It was too much of a coincidence. It looked like a mark placed on purpose.

In the afternoon Emily returned, unable to hide her excitement, though there was tension in her face.

"Lady Mary agreed. There is a dinner at her house tomorrow evening. Sir Reginald will be there. She will introduce us to him herself."

That meant they would meet the "philanthropist" face to face for the first time. Would he have anything to do with the Whitechapel murders.

"What about Druitt," Finn asked.

"Paul told me he is a lawyer and also teaches Latin at a boarding school," Emily said in a low voice. "He belongs to a chambers near London Bridge and goes there on Wednesdays to handle legal matters."

Finn considered and turned to Emily. "The day after to-morrow is Wednesday. We will go to that chambers and meet Druitt ourselves."

***

Night fell. They dressed properly and took a carriage to Lady Mary's house.

Belgravia shone with light; carriages lined the street, and music drifted from the hall.

Lady Mary stood at the center of the crowd, composed beneath the chandeliers. Beside her was a tall, broad man with a bald crown, glass in hand, surrounded by men of politics and commerce.

When she saw them, Lady Mary came forward to greet them warmly. Emily went to her grandparents, and Finn offered polite thanks. A brief exchange followed, then Lady Mary inclined her head toward the bald gentleman.

It was Sir Reginald Whitmore.

A quiet tension rose in Finn's chest. Even here, in the brightness of Belgravia, she could almost hear Whitechapel's fog whispering beyond the windows.

Sir Reginald turned his head. His gaze moved over the room and settled on them. A searching look flashed in his eyes, then he put on a warm smile.

"Ah, Lady Mary, and these two are…?"

41

"This is Finn Parker. She is writing a book on the cultures of London's districts. This is my niece Emily, who is helping with the materials."

Sir Reginald smiled more broadly and offered his hand, the palm thick and strong.

"Studying culture is a noble pursuit. London's soul lies in its variety."

Finn took his hand. There was a chill in it she could not name.

After thanking Lady Mary they entered the hall with Sir Reginald, glasses in hand. Gaslight broke into ripples on the crystal. Music and murmurs interwove like a thin curtain.

"Miss Parker," Sir Reginald said in a gentle tone, "you are writing on London's culture. It is not an easy subject. London has many faces. The entertainments of the upper world. The disorder of the lower streets."

He dropped his voice on the last words, almost speaking into her ear.

Finn kept her expression even. "I walked the East End a few days ago. It is indeed the city's most contradictory quarter. A market and workshops by day, and by night another world. That is why I want to set it down."

A young man approached. He was tall and well made, his features regular, his step a fraction stiff. With both hands he carried a silver case. There was a slight smile on his face and a hint of nerves, as if afraid to make a mistake. He presented a cigar to Sir Reginald with careful attention.

"Thank you, Michael," Sir Reginald said casually.

Then he spoke at ease. "Miss Parker, you really should write about youths like him. He was born in Whitechapel, raised by a single mother, and makes his own living. Now he assists me. He is a good example of how London's poor strive upward."

Whitechapel struck in Finn's mind with a sudden knock. She glanced at Michael. He did not meet her eyes. As he lit Sir Reginald's cigar, his fingers trembled slightly with nerves, then he lowered his head like an assistant careful not to trouble his master. In the crystal light his look flickered once, then sank. He stood silent, unreadable.

"He does look very young," Emily said softly.

Michael raised his eyes at once and glanced at her. Surprise crossed his gaze for a moment and was gone. He pressed it down and produced a strained smile, like a child awkward under praise.

Something moved in Finn's mind. On the surface the young man looked simple.

She only smiled a little and said nothing more. Inwardly she reckoned that if they wanted the East End's secrets, the youth named Michael might yield a few threads.

The dinner went on with laughter and the clink of glasses. Sir Reginald talked of policy and charities. Servants and guests crossed paths like a weave. Finn had already made up her mind.

As the evening neared its end, she turned to Sir Reginald on her right and spoke as if in passing. "Might I call on you one day and take down a few anecdotes. It would help my book a great deal."

"Why not tomorrow evening," he said readily. "Come to dinner at my house. You can arrive at dusk, we will talk a while, then eat together."

"Could Michael join us," Finn asked at once. "I would like to hear his view of Whitechapel."

He laughed lightly. "Very well. I will give the order. I will send a carriage for you at four tomorrow afternoon."

"Much obliged," Finn said. The Belgravia engagement for the next night was fixed.

***

The next morning Finn arranged to meet Emily near London Bridge so they could go together to Druitt's chambers. Fog lay over the Thames. Water slapped the piers. Far off, carriage wheels rattled.

It was an old building with an unobtrusive brass plate at the door listing several barristers. When the heavy wooden door swung open, dust rose with the old scent of ink.

Behind the desk in the front hall a young man looked up. His face was fair and regular, pale from long hours over the ledgers. His manner showed professional caution. His hair was a deep walnut brown that took a dull sheen in the gaslight, making his quiet reserve more evident. Finn saw the name plate on his desk. Samuel Briggs, clerk of the chambers.

"Ladies. Do you require legal advice," he asked in a flat, professional tone.

Finn took out a slip of paper and lowered her voice. "We are here for Montague John Druitt."

Briggs' brows shifted a fraction, as if something unpleasant had passed through his mind. He mastered himself at once, rose, and said briefly, "Mr Druitt is inside today, working through documents. Do you have an appointment. If not, I can announce you, but he may not see you."

"We can wait," Finn said, her tone firm.

Briggs hesitated, then opened the inner door.

Soon he returned and spoke in a low voice. "Mr Druitt will see you. This way."

They entered Druitt's office. The furnishings were spare; a few files lay neatly on the desk. He was tall and slender, ash-brown hair combed close, well dressed, with handsome features edged by pride. His eyes were keen, wary, and impatient, as if the world offended him by existing. He looked up. A professional smile touched his mouth. His tone was cool. "Please sit. What legal advice do you require."

They sat. Finn spoke evenly. "Suppose a person's notepaper is found in the homes of several victims. What can be done in law."

Druitt started, the surprise gone in an instant. He gave a cold snort. "That is not a legal problem. If you have suspicions, you should go to the police."

Finn glanced at the files on his desk, then sharpened her voice. "What if that notepaper bears your name."

The room froze.

Druitt snapped upright. His eyes turned cutting. His voice drove at them. "What do you mean by that?"

Emily added coldly, "Mary Jane Kelly, Ashley Mclany, Annette Westwood. You know them all, do you not?"

His face went stiff, then he leaned back with his arms crossed and put on contempt. "Whether I know them or not, what has that to do with you?"

Finn pressed him. "Kelly was a Ripper victim, dismembered. Ashley has been missing for weeks. A man with a knife broke into Annette's home the night before last. Your notepaper was in their rooms. Are you the man with the knife?"

Druitt started, then brought his hand down on the desk. His voice rose. "Nonsense. You go too far. How dare you burst into my office and smear my name with this drivel. I am a Winchester man. My qualification is clean. I will not have this."

Finn said in a cold voice, "How do you explain your notepaper in their homes?"

A flicker crossed his face, but he held the arrogant pose. "I do not know what you are talking about."

Emily cut in, her voice like ice. "I have been told those three attended private dinners in Belgravia arranged by you. Carriages, fees, all through your hands."

Finn followed at once. "Shall I go to Scotland Yard now and state this. Think. If you are detained, your name will be on the front page of every paper in London. Can you bear it?"

Druitt laughed. "So. You only know how to threaten? What law forbids introductions? I know them and have found them work. The wealthy need cleaners and servers. I make the introductions. Yes, I take a fee. Is that a crime. If you mean to blacken me, go ahead."

His tone stayed hard, the pose unassailable.

Finn's thought shifted. She said coolly, "It would not be a coincidence if you knew the other four victims as well, would it?"

Druitt's expression jerked. Something flashed in his eyes. He forced out, "Leave."

They went straight outside and crossed the wet stones to wait in a tavern opposite. As expected, before long Druitt hurried out and took a hansom cab.

Emily followed in her own carriage while Finn returned to the Mayfair house to put the material in order and asked the porter to have a boy carry a note to Paul. If they were to trace Druitt's ties to the other four victims, they would need a visit to the East End magistrates' court.

The carriage jolted along the slick stones. Emily watched through the curtain, eyes fixed on Druitt's four-wheeler. When they crossed the cold wind on the bridge and turned into wide streets, her heart sank. They were not going east but toward Belgravia. A moment later the carriage slowed near Eaton Place. Druitt alighted, spoke in a low voice with an older butler at the portico, and was led into the house.

Emily fixed the time, the number, and the route in her mind. She did not go closer. She turned her carriage and went back to Mayfair for Finn.

"He went to Sir Reginald's house," Emily said as soon as she entered, pale.

Finn nodded steadily and they changed clothes in haste. Before four, with their shawls still warm, the porter announced that Sir Reginald's carriage had arrived.

Before they got in, Finn and Emily went over their accounts and questions again and lined up their doubts. Druitt's notepaper. The private dinners in Belgravia. O'Leary's well-dressed gentleman.

***

They were set down at the Whitmore residence. The butler approached with respect.

"Sir Reginald is in the study speaking with a visitor and cannot receive you at once. You may wait in the library. If you prefer, you may go to the morning room or the drawing room."

Finn and Emily chose the library. A run of gilt spines shone softly in the gaslight. The fire whispered in the grate. The silver tea tray trembled faintly. The room was quiet and decorous.

Before long Sir Reginald entered, composed, as if he had only exchanged polite words in the study.

"Miss Parker, it is an honor to see you beyond the study door," he said with polished courtesy. "If anything I have seen can serve your book on London's culture, I am glad to offer it."

Light talk began with music, charities, and veterans' funds. The atmosphere was just right. When Finn brought up the East End, he took the thread himself and dropped his voice.

"Whitechapel. The city's wound."

He paused before going on. "You must have heard of the Ripper. I knew Mary Jane Kelly. At times a charity watched over her. I and several acquaintances did what we could. Her misfortune still troubles me."

As he spoke there was a trace of sorrow in his eyes, as if mourning an unattended soul. Emily lowered her lashes, moved by his show of pity. Finn noted how careful his wording was, the boundary held to near perfection. He knew Kelly, but not closely. He cared for the East End, but did not enter it. Each word shaved to shape, smooth and safe.

From the end of the corridor a low voice carried, suppressed but hot.

Michael came in quietly, greeted them, then bent at Sir Reginald's ear and spoke in a whisper. Finn held her breath to listen. "Druitt has just left," he said. Sir Reginald nodded to him.

Finn decided to test him and raised an old Whitechapel story as if by chance. "Speaking of Whitechapel, Sir Reginald, I recently heard an Irishman's tale. He is called O'Leary and lives near Spitalfields Market. They say he witnessed details of a Ripper case and was nearly silenced. Have you, or Michael, heard of this. Since Michael is from there, he might have heard something from the neighbors."

Michael's eyes flickered. His breath quickened for an instant. He lowered his head and answered Finn in a very low tone. "I have been away from Whitechapel a long time, miss. Those street tales, I do not know them well." His voice was steady.

Finn thought, so he knows of O'Leary. The flicker was too plain, as if he were avoiding something.

Sir Reginald seemed not to notice. He motioned for Michael to stay. "He knows the East End. He may be able to offer you some information."

Michael sat opposite Finn with careful manners. "There is little to say of the East End," he said gently. "But I did grow up there. The streets are always wet. Children idle at the corners. Many cannot get into proper schools. At night there are often quarrels or screams. For us that is ordinary."

His tone was cautious and his face showed little change. The words sounded sincere and yet seemed deliberately spare, each one leaving room to turn, making him hard to read.

Finn took the chance to praise him. "Sir Reginald has a good eye to find a bright youth like you."

Michael smiled a little and looked to Sir Reginald. "Sir Reginald took me in," he said with a hint of eagerness, "so I could live here and study. When the secretary has leave I sometimes help with Sir's affairs."

"How did you come to know Sir Reginald?" Finn asked.

Michael started and looked again to Sir Reginald. Sir Reginald narrowed his eyes and returned the look over his cigar. Michael said unwillingly, "A lawyer introduced me to Sir Reginald."

Finn watched him and asked, "Was the lawyer Druitt." Druitt's tie to Sir Reginald seemed more than slight.

Michael paused and only after a moment nodded. "Yes. Do you know him?"

Finn nodded and explained half truthfully, half not. "I have met many people for the book. He is often in the magistrates' court and knows those from Whitechapel."

Sir Reginald took the line with a brightness that seemed overly polished. "Michael is a good lad. He learns quickly. He had little schooling when young, but I saw at once he was not ordinary, so I kept him and gave him the chance to study. He is now my right hand and can handle anything. I have always supported the East End church charities and hope to help Whitechapel's children when I can."

He went on. "What the East End needs is order and opportunity, not rumor chasing. The papers like to paint a story. The real work is often unseen."

He looked at Finn and softened his voice to an appeal. "Let your book write hope, not only fear."

Finn answered with polite phrases, letting her thoughts arrange themselves.

Druitt, his ties to the women were clear. Emily had seen him enter this house, and he had likely just been in the study, arguing with someone. Yet he might still be only a scapegoat, placed to draw attention away.

Michael, outwardly modest, movements restrained, words respectful. But he shrank from mention of his past, and there was something too careful in the way he spoke, as though composure itself were a mask.

Sir Reginald, posture flawless, each word measured. Even his admission, *I knew Kelly*, sounded rehearsed, polished into pity. The refinement seemed too deliberate, and his link with Druitt made Finn wonder whether his hands, too, were somewhere in the Ripper's shadow.

At dinner Finn and Emily were invited to the dining room. Candles wavered along the long table. Silver gleamed. The dishes were refined and abundant. Sir Reginald's cook was clearly a master. The talk did not return to Finn's book. He showed interest in her background. She mentioned her childhood and youth in Chicago and touched briefly on her family. He listened with steady interest and perfect manners.

When they rose from table, Sir Reginald escorted them to the front portico himself. To Finn's surprise, Michael held the reins. He sat in the coachman's place and lifted his hat politely when he saw her. Finn returned the gesture.

The carriage rattled over the wet stones and drew up at Number 12, Mayfair. Gaslight warmed the porch, touching red brick and white stone. Iron balconies caught the light, and lamps on either side of the portico gleamed on the brass knocker and bell.

The porter opened the door with a bow. Inside, marble and polished brass reflected the stairwell's steady glow. The red carpet softened her steps, and the quiet order of the place carried a sense of safety.

Finn was about to say good night to Michael when he jumped down from the coachman's seat and came quickly after them. His tone was as respectful as ever, with a firmness that allowed no refusal.

"Pardon me, ladies. Sir's orders. I am to make sure you enter safely with my own eyes."

Emily started and answered under her breath, "There is no need. There is a porter here. We will be fine."

Michael kept his head lowered and spoke with earnestness that bordered on stubbornness. "Sir Reginald was most particular. I cannot disobey."

With such insistence they let him escort them up the stairs. The corridor was very quiet. Only their steps pressed the red carpet. At the flat door he checked the lock for them, then stepped back and lifted his hat.

"May you sleep well," he said softly. His eyes glinted for a moment in the gaslight, then dropped as he withdrew into the shadow.

Finn and Emily looked at each other and said nothing. Sir Reginald was thorough indeed.

Chapter Four

Early the next morning the porter rang the brass bell.

Jessica came quickly up the stairs and handed Finn a letter. The paper was thin. The handwriting was hurried.

"Twelve o'clock today. Fleet Street tavern. You must come, Paul."

Finn's chest tightened. She looked up at Emily. Emily had read it too. Her eyes caught the light as she whispered, "He must have found something."

Before noon the gas lamps had not fully gone out. Fog still hung in the street.

The tavern smelled of beer, ink, and old newsprint. A few editors murmured over the latest morning edition.

Paul was already at a window table. He looked tired, but there was a brightness he could not hide in his eyes. When he saw them, he pressed the papers in his coat onto the table and lowered his voice.

"I paid a price." He paused and glanced around. "A junior copyist at the magistrates' court owes me a favor. He let me see a few registers that should not have left the shelves."

He dropped his voice further, more cautious than before. "But before I begin, you tell me why you were asking about the barrister Montague John Druitt."

Finn met Emily's eyes, then said, "A model in my art class told me she met Kelly and Ashley at a private dinner. That dinner was arranged by this barrister. But you must not mention her name to anyone. I am afraid she is in danger."

Paul's brow moved. He nodded and accepted that. He pushed a creased stack of pages across and spoke with a weight like lead. "The records show that those women who died in the East End, Mary Jane Kelly, Annie Chapman, Elizabeth Stride, Catherine Eddowes, and the missing Ashley and Annette, all sought the same barrister for defense while alive."

Finn and Emily understood at once. "It was… Druitt?"

Paul nodded heavily. "Yes."

His breathing quickened a little, though his tone stayed controlled. "It is not one or two names. It is every known victim. Such overlap cannot be explained by coincidence."

His knuckles tapped the table, as if tamping down a surge of excitement. "This is a very strong lead. If I print it outright, it will be called rumor chasing. I will verify it from another angle. Druitt's movements and associations, whether there are deeper ties between him and these women?"

He paused and added, "You said just now he did arrange for Kelly and Ashley to attend private dinners. Perhaps that is the starting point."

He looked up suddenly and pressed his voice lower. "Is your model friend safe now? Still in Whitechapel?"

Finn shook her head. "I have settled her at the Brown Hotel. I do not dare let her return for now."

Paul's expression eased a little, then he pressed on. "The young female corpse you asked me to find last time. Was that Ashley? Any result?"

Emily answered, "There have been three young women found dead in Whitechapel over the past two months. We examined each case. The first drowned in the Thames and washed ashore at Wapping. The second died of an opium overdose, no knife wounds."

She hesitated. "The third died of suffocation. Marks on the neck, faint traces of a blade at the throat, no deeper cut. The report called it strangulation. To me, it looked unfinished."

Paul jotted a few notes and frowned. "So all three died unnaturally, yet none fits the Ripper's pattern."

Emily lowered her lashes, her voice barely above a whisper. "We suspected the third for a time, but the coroner wrote death by strangulation, assailant unknown. The police statements and the papers turned it into gossip, calling it a suspected romantic dispute."

Finn added, "In other words, Ashley's whereabouts are still unknown. She may be dead and not yet identified. Or she may be alive and hidden away."

Paul let out a long breath and pressed down the agitation in his chest. "If she is hidden, it means she knows something. The more she knows, the greater the danger."

Emily murmured, "But why would he kill them?"

Paul kept his voice low. "A serial killer may act from character defects or childhood injury. This kind of man often needs no fixed motive. He only needs opportunity."

He paused, his gaze as if trying to cut through the fog. "You have been tracking the Ripper, have you not?" He turned to Finn at once. "The book is only your pretext? Is that so?"

Finn gave no answer. With Paul's nose for exclusives he was like a shark to blood. She also knew that with his help, information would be easier to obtain.

After a moment she said, "Can you find a way to get Druitt's client lists?"

Paul looked up sharply and fixed his eyes on her. "You think Druitt is suspicious. And that he will go on killing."

Finn kept steady. "I think it is worth tracing his clients. Whether he himself is suspect is too early to say?"

She added, "I worry that some of those clients have already met with harm." She opened a page of her notebook. "The first confirmed Ripper case was Mary Ann Nichols on August thirty-first. I suspect that before Mary, the Ripper had already practiced more than once."

Emily drew a breath. "So the Ripper could not restrain himself? That is why he sent letters to the papers and to the Whitechapel Vigilance Committee?"

Finn considered. "If those victims are tied to Druitt, could someone be framing him? An enemy of his? What hatred would it take to avenge oneself by serial murder upon the innocent? Or else Druitt is very deliberate. He understands how to balance false and true and set the board himself?"

Emily's eyes widened and she blurted out, "We at least know the killer is a slender man."

Paul followed at once. "How do you know that."

Emily flushed. Finn judged it was time to tell Paul what they had. She laid out how she had lodged at Annette's house to learn about Whitechapel, how she had found Druitt's notepaper in the homes of Annette, Kelly, and Ashley, how Emily had gone to Whitechapel alone out of fear for Finn's safety, and how she had been attacked that night. She did not yet mention O'Leary or the barman.

Paul kept composed. When he heard of the break-in, he frowned at Emily and only after a moment said, "If something had happened to you, how do you expect us to go on."

Emily stepped forward and embraced him. "I am sorry, Uncle. I will be careful. I will not be reckless again."

He turned to Finn. "Are you not afraid? Walking about at midnight."

"Of course I am," Finn said. "I have trained since childhood. I can defend myself. But I was wrong to give Emily such a fright."

"That was her choice. She was very bold, and we are lucky she is unharmed." Paul went on, "So you believe the man with the knife that night was the Ripper?"

"Yes," Finn said. "He moved quickly. The knife shone with intent. He had been lying in wait outside the window. His target was Annette from the start. Even if Emily had not opened the window, he would have pried it with a tool. And when he saw Emily's clothes and face, he clearly started. I believe his true target was Annette."

Paul said, "Let us assume the man was the Ripper and the target was Annette. You linked Kelly and Annette by the private dinners of Sir Reginald and then added Ashley to the list. These people happen to be Druitt's clients." He paused. "Yesterday was Wednesday. Did you go to him?"

Emily said, "We did. We confronted him. He admitted he had introduced clients to work and admitted he knew Kelly, Ashley, and Annette. Soon after meeting us he hurried to Sir Reginald's house, but I do not know what passed there."

Finn added, "Emily and I were introduced to Sir Reginald by Lady Mary. I used the book as my pretext and called on him yesterday afternoon. Druitt was at the house then."

"You move quickly. You have already seen so many people," Paul said, incredulous. "But you still cannot be sure whether Sir Reginald is tied to the cases of these young women?"

Finn said, "Sir Reginald should be on the list of suspects."

Emily said, "He is older and stout. He does not look like the killer."

Finn smiled at that. "But he is connected."

She asked in a steady tone, "Paul, is it normal for an ordinary barrister to receive so many cases?"

Paul hesitated, thought crossing his brow. "In principle a case goes first through a solicitor, then through the chambers clerk who assigns it to a barrister. For Druitt to receive so many over time is unusual. Perhaps his clerk has ties with a few solicitors and they look after one another, so cases often land in his hands. This is not rare in the trade. I can inquire and see whether it is tied to his clerk."

Finn nodded. She had a first outline of how English law moved. "But how can people in Whitechapel afford a barrister for defense?"

Paul answered, "That puzzled me too, so I made inquiries. The Whitechapel parish established a charity fund that pays for defense for the poor. Donors include Lady Mary and Sir Reginald, and my parents as well. They give regularly."

Finn thought, was this the 'mercy fund' Sir Reginald mentioned yesterday.

Emily put in, "I think I have attended those charity dinners. They were very dull."

Paul said, "It would help if we could hear from someone who knows Druitt and how the chambers work."

Emily thought for a moment. "In that case, let me approach a barrister at Druitt's chambers. I can pretend to be interested in legal work and see what he will say. Grandfather's friend, Sir Edward Latham, is a barrister. I can claim I wish to learn the profession. As for how to meet, I will ask my uncle's staff to make the introduction."

Paul hesitated. "Barristers may not easily disclose anything. Their duty is to keep matters private." He paused, then added, "Perhaps it would be better to approach someone from the general staff instead?"

Emily's eyes brightened. "Then I can speak to the clerk we met last time."

Paul nodded. "That seems the wiser choice. How will you approach him?"

Emily smiled, though her tone was serious. "I will tell Sir Edward that I wish to learn about a clerk's duties. To others, I will simply say I have taken a liking to the clerk and wish to meet him."

Finn looked at her, admiring and worried in equal measure.

Paul thought for a moment, then nodded slowly. "All right. The clerk is a real opening. But you must be careful."

The table fell quiet. Only the scratch of a pen on paper remained. He circled the last word, then gathered the papers and looked up with a cold, sharp gaze.

"We split up from here. I will review Druitt's past court cases and see whom else he defended, then try to confirm whether those clients are still alive. I only hope the copyist does not grow suspicious. If this leaks, Druitt will at once become the city's enemy. The police will be glad to make him a scapegoat. I want the truth, not headlines. If he is the Ripper, exposing him now will only drive him deeper, for the proof is too thin."

Finn nodded. Paul went on, "Emily, you start with the clerk. Learn what you can of Druitt's private life."

Finn said, "I want to look more closely at Sir Reginald and his assistant, Michael. Leave that to us. Come dine at my house this week. We will gather the latest results then."

Paul tapped his knuckle lightly on the table and lowered his voice. "Be careful in all things."

"The Fleet Street editors are waiting for me," he said, closing his notebook and pulling his hat brim down. "Tomorrow night."

He rose, put on his coat, and his figure slipped into the fog boiling at the tavern door.

Finn and Emily looked at one another and said nothing. The beating in their chests reminded them that this was only the beginning.

***

After they left the tavern, Emily went to contact Sir Edward Latham to arrange a meeting. Finn returned to Whitechapel. At the London Hospital she presented herself as a representative of the Whitechapel church charity fund and was allowed into the ward. O'Leary's wound had been stitched. Black thread pulled at swollen skin, the long gash alarming to see. It should have killed him. The bleeding Finn had stanched that night had pulled him back from the edge. She set down fruit and restoratives and spoke first of public order in Whitechapel and of his lodgings, then moved the subject to the night of the attack. His memory of that night was in pieces. He recalled being brought to the hospital door and had always thought himself assaulted in the street.

Finn pursued another line and asked whether he had arranged to meet anyone. After a long pause he remembered running into an old neighbor, Matthew, at the market. Matthew said he had returned with great difficulty and arranged to call at nine that night to talk over old times. Because of the attack he never kept the appointment and felt deep regret. The memory rose from the fog with a slow sadness. Finn believed that the letters signed "M" in O'Leary's rooms were Matthew. The old story of the mother's death and the boy who vanished matched the neighbors' accounts.

Later she returned to his lodgings again and found the same box. A few clumsy practice notes lay inside, intimate in tone, and addressed to "Uncle O."

At dusk she made inquiries at a corner with an old neighbor. The boy had been poor, sold newspapers, and ran errands for the slaughterhouse. His mother drank and beat him. A grocer's young master bullied him and even broke his little finger. Later the boy pushed him down a stair. After the mother died the boy suddenly disappeared. People thought the church had sent him away.

By the years he would now be just over twenty. The old grocery had long since changed hands more than once.

***

With Sir Edward's help, Emily secured a luncheon with Samuel Briggs at a tavern near London Bridge. When she arrived, he was already waiting. He rose at once to greet her and did not sit again until the waiter pulled out her chair.

"Good to see you, Emily. I did not expect we would meet again so soon," Samuel said kindly.

"Thank you for taking the time. I truly want to understand how a chambers runs," Emily said with a smile. "I can see you are very capable. The work must demand a great deal."

Samuel did not answer the compliment directly. He only smiled at her. "It is an honor to dine with you. Sir Edward holds a lofty place in the law. His firm is where every clerk and counsel dreams of working." His tone was even, with a slight edge. "Although one of his solicitors arranged this lunch, I suppose Sir Edward has some tie to you. In London the name Ashcroft carries considerable weight. Why not ask his firm directly? Why come to a chambers clerk?"

The words were mild, but the phrasing carried a blade. Emily was prepared and did not lose her composure. "Sir Edward is my uncle. The people in his firm listen to him. Whatever they tell me will be polished and meant to make me give up the idea." She smiled sweetly, but there was resolve in her tone. "You are different. You look like a man of principle. You will not flatter anyone and talk against your conscience. I believe you will tell me plainly."

Samuel smiled, pleased by her words. "I am happy to answer your questions."

The waiter brought hot lamb pies and beer. Samuel set his knife and fork in order and began slowly. "Becoming a clerk is not about book learning as you imagine. Our trade rests on endurance, not degrees. Most start at twelve or thirteen, running errands in chambers, messages, copying, odd jobs. I was no different. I had no background and had to work early. I was fortunate to have a steady hand and passable arithmetic. Bit by bit I handled copies and files and learned the flow of legal work. Later our senior clerk moved to this chambers. He valued me and brought me over as an assistant clerk. You could say I am here through diligence and through connections."

He glanced up at Emily. There was pride in his tone, but it did not boast. "Now I receive solicitors, pass briefs to suitable barristers, and keep the business moving. Above me is the senior clerk. He controls the whole chambers' trade. Whoever takes which case ends with his say."

He paused and cut a piece of pie, then spoke with the calm of fact. "Our chambers is among the larger ones in London. We have several well-known barristers. To outsiders they are the leads on the stage. Clerks like us are the cogs that make the stage turn."

Emily turned her glass and watched him closely. "How do you see the work."

Samuel was quiet for a moment. His eyes rested on the beer as if weighing how much to say. At last he spoke softly. "At times it feels heavy. Outsiders see only the barristers' shine in court. They do not know how much of the petty and the pressure we bear behind it. Sources, favors, money, all press on us. This work gives me a place to stand. It also reminds me without end that the light on the stage is never ours. The leads get the applause. We hold the stage up in silence."

Emily felt a stir. She heard the tension in his voice. Endurance, and a resignation that could not be said outright.

Her expression softened. She set her glass down and spoke with a gentle firmness. "You are right. Many people run behind the scenes and never stand in the light. You are where you are because of effort and skill. Not everyone can endure, and not everyone has the nerve to reach. You should be proud to sit here."

Samuel's smile showed gratitude. It seemed a shadow had been brushed from his heart, though a faint loneliness lingered.

After a while Emily probed, "When we went to see Druitt the other day, did he say why."

Samuel looked interested. "After you left, I asked whether I should enter it in the book. He said you contacted him on private business."

"Is that what he said?" Emily sounded amused.

"Is it not so?" Samuel asked.

"In a way. It was private. It concerns a book on London's culture. My roommate Finn is researching. We heard Druitt has experience with cases in Whitechapel, so we wanted his insights." Emily offered the reason she had prepared. "We were probably rude. We should have made an appointment. We went in our excitement."

"No wonder you left so soon," Samuel said, thoughtful. "You want to learn about the East End."

"Yes. Whether it is as crime-ridden as people say," Emily said, choosing words as positively as she could. "We also want to interview counsel who handle cases from White-chapel. Druitt does take many cases from there. Is that why he is often assigned?"

Samuel was quiet and considered. "That plays a part. But every assignment is decided by the senior clerk. Since Druitt has that experience, it is easier to send him those briefs."

"So he does not seek them out himself," Emily asked.

"He would like more briefs all the same," Samuel said, musing.

"Do barristers like court assignments. I thought people in Whitechapel could not pay much," Emily said.

Samuel nodded. "Yes. The church fund pays. The fees are much lower than ordinary cases. Our chambers does a little good and gives our counsel some income. Young barristers like these cases because they build experience and bring in a bit of money."

"But Druitt is quite experienced, is he not? Then he is very charitable to keep taking them," Emily said.

Samuel showed a brief look of disdain, but it passed at once. "Druitt is a decent man," he said, unconvincingly.

Emily let it pass. The table grew quiet for a moment. Only the chime of knives and forks remained.

"If I really pursued a clerk's assistant path, would I need lessons in typing and such," Emily asked.

"If you have skills like that, it helps you get hired," Samuel said, a little awkward. "But you need not fear. You have uncles to back you."

Emily pretended to take offense. "Perhaps I will apply at another firm."

Samuel smiled and said nothing more.

Lunch ended in a friendly air.

When Emily returned, Finn asked, "How was lunch with Samuel."

Emily nodded, then smiled. "You probably would not like him."

Finn raised a brow for her to go on.

"He is a little full of himself and proud of what he has achieved, with that air you dislike, certain of his own judgment," Emily said. "But to be fair, I think he is interesting. He is very proud of the clerk's role in chambers. He thinks he is the force behind those better-read barristers and that he holds the power to direct cases. It is a pride that can grate. But with his background, I imagine he did not grow up well off, and to become an assistant clerk at his age is no small thing."

Finn watched her with interest.

A faint color rose in Emily's cheeks. "He did mention Uncle Sir Edward often, but he was polite throughout and never fawned like other men. He answered questions directly and behaved properly. I seldom meet a man so proper."

Finn nodded. With Emily's looks and station, she never lacked admirers. A man who could be alone with her and keep within bounds was new to her.

Emily paused, then grew serious. "To the point. I am sure Druitt receives so many cases mostly because of the clerk's assignments. His practice is not especially strong. One thing puzzles me. Samuel spoke with pride at first about directing case flow as assistant clerk. When I pressed him on why Druitt always gets court briefs, he pushed it off as the senior clerk's decision. The two answers do not quite match."

Finn did not reply at once. Emily spoke up in his defense. "Perhaps he did not want to sound like boasting."

***

Night fell. The Mayfair flat glowed warm. Gas shades softened the light. Heavy curtains shut out the fog and the sound of wheels. The fire in the grate cracked and filled the hall with a gentle heat.

The table was laid with white linen. Silver and crystal were set in order. The home supper was planned by their cook, Karen. It was not a grand feast, but it was tasteful and exact. The courses were these, A cream of pumpkin soup to start, sprinkled with fresh nutmeg and feathered with cream, with warm wheat bread alongside. The main was beef braised in red wine, tender and rich, with root vegetables, and a bottle of Bordeaux. Last came an almond pudding with caramel sauce, fragrant and lingering.

Finn lifted her glass and smiled. "Before we share our findings, let us taste Karen's work. After the main course we will lay out our threads one by one. Shall we."

Paul nodded at once, raised his glass, and spoke low with a certain gravity. "To our good company."

When they had finished the main, Emily spoke first and relayed her lunch, especially Samuel's account of a clerk's duties. "On one hand he says he can steer the flow of cases. When it comes to Druitt he pushes it to the senior clerk. He clearly does not want to be nailed down."

"Did he say anything else about Druitt," Paul asked.

"His business is not especially strong, so he accepts East End cases for a little income," Emily said, then added, "He also said Druitt is a decent man, but it sounded hollow to me."

"Perhaps he senses another side of Druitt," Finn said softly. "They are colleagues. They spend time together. It is not strange that he notices."

They fell silent for a time. Only the delicate sounds of silver on porcelain remained.

After a while Paul spoke again with weight. "The copyist who owes me a favor, the one I mentioned, copied all of Druitt's court cases for me. So he would not grow suspicious, I also asked him to pull registers for several other barristers in the chambers. Because of that I found that Druitt's assignments are two to three times the others'. Very suspicious. What is his tie to the clerks."

He drew a small notebook from his coat and went on. "I focused on the list of clients from Whitechapel. Some are confirmed. Most are theft or affray. Your friend Annette and the missing Ashley are on it. Some are no longer where they used to be. They may have moved. Or, as we suspected, they have met with harm."

He stopped and his gaze darkened. "If we find the missing in the register of unknown dead, we may have a duty to give the names to the police. It would mean those clients are already on the roll of the dead. They are in great danger. I would very much like the exclusive."

"In that case, Druitt's name will be ruined. He may not be the killer, but he will not be able to wash his hands of it," Paul added. "And O'Leary did say that on the night Kelly died he saw a well-dressed gentleman on Dorset Street. The public will suspect him, however the wind blows."

Finn set down her silver and spoke more quietly. "I must admit something." She briefly told how she had posed as a representative of the Whitechapel church fund to visit O'Leary in the hospital. He had spoken of an old neighbor, Matthew, from whom he had been parted for more than seven years, who had arranged to call that night to talk over old times, an appointment missed because of the attack.

"O'Leary always thought himself attacked in the street, but it seems less simple. That Matthew may give us another line." She added, "I meant to press him about the well-dressed gentleman he saw on Dorset Street, but he was too weak and soon slept. Earlier a barman told me O'Leary had mentioned another man walking with that gentleman."

She paused and lowered her voice. "When I tried to contact the barman again he had disappeared."

They looked at one another. A close, repressed tension filled the air.

Paul spoke first. "We split the work. I will confirm one by one who on the list is still alive. Those unaccounted for, I will compare against the unknown dead." He turned to Emily. "You find a way to draw more from Samuel. See whether he knows the tie between the clerks and Druitt. I think Druitt's flow of court cases may link to the Ripper. He knows more than he shows."

At last he looked at Finn. "You must trace Matthew, the one O'Leary named. He may be more crucial than any of us think."

Finn nodded, her face set. "All right. I also want to look deeper into Sir Reginald and his assistant, Michael. After all, Druitt went to see him suddenly after meeting us. Sir Reginald is at least linked to Kelly, Ashley, and Annette. He may know the others as well."

Paul picked up the line. "This Michael, you said he is from Whitechapel, from a single-mother home, young. That sounds a little like Matthew."

Finn and Emily both drew a breath, then slowly nodded. Emily spoke at last. "Although Michael seems polite, I do not know why, but when I passed him at Sir Reginald's house I felt a sudden fear. It may only be my fear of Belgravia."

The glasses chimed faintly in the lamplight, but no one spoke. The careful yet heavy supper ended under a hush. The three had each taken up a difficult task.

Chapter Five

On Paul's list, Finn found a court record from 1881. It concerned a thirteen-year-old defendant charged with assault after pushing a neighbor from the second floor. The plaintiff was Kelvin Baker, aged thirty-two, and the defense was conducted by Montague John Druitt, then a pupil barrister. The defendant's name had been struck through, the judge having ordered it withheld. By custom, records involving minors were not kept for long, and only a brief note of the case remained.

Finn thought to herself. If the boy was Matthew, he would be twenty now, about Michael's age. After his mother died seven years ago, did he take refuge with Druitt? Then did Druitt refer him to Sir Reginald, and his life turned aside from there? The person O'Leary meant to meet that night, could it have been him? And could he be the hand in the dark with the knife?

If so, did he strike because O'Leary recognized him on Dorsett Street? Could he be the Ripper? But then why target people tied to Druitt?

The questions gathered, all of them conjecture.

Finn shook her head. Michael was, after all, the only man from Whitechapel she knew. She had to stay objective and not force him into the shape of Matthew.

She had to confirm Michael's origins before she tested the rest.

That afternoon, after her art class, Finn returned home and wrote a letter by hand. She asked the maid to give it to the porter to deliver to Sir Reginald's house, hoping he would spare time to see her and let her supplement details for her book.

***

The next day Sir Reginald's reply arrived. He invited her to take tea that afternoon and said he would have Michael present so she could ask him for details if needed.

Finn went first to the London Hospital to see O'Leary. He was weak but able to speak with effort. She asked him to recall and describe the Matthew he had met at the market and the "well-dressed gentleman" he had seen on Dorsett Street. She kept quiet watch at his bedside and after three hours finished two portraits.

The portrait of Matthew was easier. O'Leary remembered him clearly. "Of middling height, spare in build, though the shoulders had filled out with work. Hair dark brown, catching a reddish hue in sunlight. A plain face, open and steady, the jaw well shaped. Eyes gray-blue, thoughtful, not quick. Nose straight, skin fair but roughened by weather.

Wore a laborer's coat that day, decent and clean. Looked like someone who'd earned his steadiness."

Finn followed his account, picturing a young man of modest birth, steady, practical, self-contained.

The "well-dressed gentleman" took him longer to recall. "Taller, perhaps, though slighter through the frame. Hair light brown, close-cut, neat as his clothes. A longer face, finer at the cheekbones, the mouth set with control. Eyes pale, maybe gray, maybe a faded blue, quick and alert. The nose a touch high, the skin smooth, never touched by sun. Spoke and moved like a man accustomed to command. The light was poor that night, but even then I knew he wasn't one of us."

The lines under her hand cleared until the image showed a man of presence hidden in the dark.

When she finished, Finn passed both portraits to O'Leary. He studied them for a long time and at last nodded.

"Is this right," she asked.

"Yes. Very like him," O'Leary said in a hoarse voice.

To Finn's eye, both Druitt and Michael could match the two faces.

As she was leaving, O'Leary caught her sleeve and asked in a low voice, "What do you want with Matthew's portrait?"

She smiled. "The church heard he has returned. They are glad and want to find him again."

He was quiet for a moment and murmured, "If you see him, tell him I am sorry. I missed our night."

Finn nodded and gave her word.

She arrived at Sir Reginald's house at the appointed hour. This time he received her himself and led her into the drawing room.

Fresh scones, soft cream, and delicate sandwiches lay on the table, all from the house cook, warm and fragrant. Under the gaslight the silver and china shone.

By Sir Reginald's order Michael waited quietly to one side, ready to refill tea or offer a cigar. His manner was deferential and he spoke little.

When the tea had run its course, Finn asked in passing, for her book's research, about East End charities.

"The people of Whitechapel are laboring folk," Sir Reginald said with a steady air. "Day to day they work for their meals. Without our funds they often will not see a doctor or send their children to school. Some would rather go to jail than pay for counsel."

"You have indeed given much to the East," Finn said with sincerity, then asked with a light smile, "Besides Michael, do you also prefer to hire staff from there. Coachmen, cooks, cleaners."

Sir Reginald smiled a little. "The trustees and I not only hire East End residents. We encourage our acquaintances to do the same. For instance, the cook you just praised is from Whitechapel. When the household staff are on leave, I hire East End hands for the day. But." He spread his hands. "The butler and Michael must often keep a closer watch. I do not say they will surely steal, only that care is needed." The words held a trace of hauteur.

Finn nodded as if in agreement and asked casually, "Are most of these people placed by the church. I have heard that Mr. Druitt sometimes introduces Whitechapel people to gentlemen."

A flicker of stiffness passed over his face, then he steadied and smiled. "You are very well informed. If there are special requests that one cannot decently state to the church, we ask Druitt to help. I, for example, prefer that a maid be fair and comely. It is awkward to say such a thing to a rector."

Finn felt a shift within. So Druitt did serve as a hidden go-between.

"Your service to the East is admirable," she said easily, "not only in giving money, but in hiring them yourself." She turned to the point. "But someone as able as Michael cannot be common."

Sir Reginald nodded with care. "Indeed. He is quick and diligent, and his response is sharp. Many servants cannot follow ten words. He knows my meaning before I have finished one."

"In that case, he must have few days off," Finn said with a light question.

At that moment she reached for her teacup and let a yellowed slip fall from her handbag, a torn scrap from O'Leary's house, signed "M," in a child's hand.

She bent to pick it up and left it a heartbeat on the table. When Michael's gaze fell on the writing his pupils tightened.

His fingers went rigid on the rim of the silver cigar case. He smoothed his face at once and returned to the pose of the respectful aide, but the pause had been too plain, like a nerve struck by the past.

Finn weighed it at once. If he was Matthew, the slip must mean much to him. If he was not, why the alertness and not simple curiosity. This was more than instinct now. It was a sign that could be traced.

Sir Reginald noticed nothing. He added mildly, "He has Sundays free. If I am away, he may also see to private errands."

"You are generous, Sir," Finn said with a pleasant smile.

From this call she fixed two points. Druitt was in truth a broker between the upper ranks and the East. And Michael had the chance to be in Whitechapel's markets at any time.

***

Emily returned to the flat a little earlier than Finn. She had just taken off her coat when a note and several papers arrived from Paul. The note held a list he had compiled from families' and neighbors' accounts of missing women. He asked them to compare the list against the unknown bodies.

Margaret Cooper, twenty-seven, medium build, dark hair, a small mole on the left cheek, missing in early August on Whitechapel Road.

Elizabeth Hill, twenty-five, blonde with blue eyes, a missing tooth shows when she smiles, disappeared in late July on Commercial Street.

Fanny Brown, thirty, full figure, both hands thick with callus from long labor, last seen at Spitalfields Market.

Catherine Williams, only twenty-one, small, black hair and green eyes, last seen on Dorset Street.

Lucy Walker, thirty-six, dark brown hair, high nose bridge, a knife scar on the right forefinger, reportedly seen on Whitechapel High Street in early August.

The oldest was Ada Miller, forty-five, thin and gray-haired, said to cough often, missing in early August on Hanbury Street.

Finn and Emily set the papers beside the coroner's reports and compared in silence. Night deepened. The lamp threw long shadows. The names on the pages read like lines of unfinished prayer.

Finn's heartbeat quickened. This was the key break. She lifted her pen at once and wrote to Paul, asking him to come that night to plan the next step.

While they waited, she passed the two portraits to Emily. "In the rush I forgot to show you. These are the two from O'Leary's account. One is Matthew. The other is the gentleman seen on Dorset Street."

Emily studied the well-dressed gentleman and spoke with care. "He looks very much like Druitt."

Finn nodded. The likeness was real. With the list of the missing, his suspicion grew heavier.

"And the other," Finn asked.

Emily frowned lightly and spoke detail by detail. "Deep brown hair. A square face. Blue eyes. A high nose bridge. Fair skin with weathering." She added in a low voice, "Like Michael."

"I think so too," Finn said.

The bell rang. The maid brought Paul into the sitting room.

After brief greetings he could not wait. "Do we have results."

Emily handed him the set. "The features of these unknown dead match the missing. The places they were found are near where they were last seen."

Paul spread the sheets and examined them closely. After a moment he looked up. His eyes were lit and his face had flushed. "Once in print, this will shake all London."

Paul went on. "If Druitt has anatomy from his father being a surgeon, that would account for the Ripper's rough handling of the bodies."

Finn nodded. "He had dealings with these women and even arranged work for some." She reported her afternoon's talk with Sir Reginald.

She lifted the portrait. "And from O'Leary's account, 'he' did appear on Dorset Street on the night Kelly died."

"So we give this to the police?" Emily asked.

Finn was silent for a beat and then spoke with weight. "The police are under pressure. If we hand this over, they will arrest Druitt at once. Druitt will be branded the Ripper. He will never wash it off."

Paul thought and said, "I would be glad to report it. The paper would roar and sell. But if he runs because of my story, I will bear the blame."

Finn said, low and firm, "At least we can be sure the victims were not chosen at random. One hand killed them one by one in order."

Emily nodded and added, "Their ages and backgrounds differ, but all are East End women who live by selling their bodies."

Finn said, "If Druitt is not a fool, he would not go on killing people tied to himself."

Emily took the line. "Or he is very deep and mixes false with true to blur the eye. It would still require the police to be shrewd. Otherwise they will close the file in haste."

Finn considered and said, "If not Druitt, then someone hates him to the marrow. He knows these women will, sooner or later, link to Druitt. He strikes first with greater savagery and even writes letters to draw the press."

They all nodded.

Emily asked again, "But who has the victims' names."

Paul analyzed. "Beyond the court registers, Druitt's brokerage leaves marks. We must learn who can reach his case records and who can reach the records of the work he arranged."

Finn looked at them both and spoke slowly. "Then we should meet Druitt face to face."

In the end they agreed to call on Montague John Druitt the next evening at Blackheath.

At dusk the next day they reached Blackheath and waited near the Valentine School. Streets ran wide and clean between tall maples and rows of red-brick terraces. White stone rails caught the last of the light. The passersby were well dressed. Shop windows set out fine pastry and silk. The air was fresh, touched with evening warmth and a quiet sense of order.

So as not to draw notice, they did not stop Druitt outside the school. They followed until impatience wore him down and he agreed to sit in a small restaurant nearby.

After drinks and a simple meal were ordered, Paul began. "I think you may know these names. Margaret Cooper, Fanny Brown, Ada Miller, Catherine Williams, Lucy Walker. Do these mean anything to you."

Druitt kept his usual arrogant air and answered Paul coolly. "I know nothing about these names."

Paul read out the reports of the unknown dead one by one.

Druitt gave a short laugh and looked at Paul. "You came again to read me the papers."

Paul smiled a little, but his voice was measured. "Besides the news, there are your court registers. These women were your clients. They disappeared in Whitechapel and now lie in the cemetery."

Druitt's laugh froze. A flicker of unease crossed his face.

Paul continued. "They share one feature. Single, female, living by the body. And each of them you stood for in court. Now they are all dead. If this reaches the police, what do you think happens. Whatever you are, your name will be bound to the Ripper."

Sweat rose on Druitt's brow. His face went from red to white and back.

Emily added, "There is testimony that on November ninth you were on Dorset Street. Tie it all together and you are almost a suspect the police could lift by the sleeve."

Druitt turned wholly pale. His voice shook. "I went there because someone asked me to deliver papers to a client's home."

Paul gave a thin smile. "Then by all means have the client speak for you."

Druitt shot back at once. "He was not at home. I left."

They looked at one another.

Finn asked gently, "Aside from court, did you meet any of these women at other times."

Druitt's hands shook as he took a notebook from his coat and turned page after page. His agitation grew.

"I must go home." He pushed up from the chair and almost fled the restaurant.

They could only watch him go. He hurried down the street to his lodgings in Blackheath.

"I would wager he will go to Sir Reginald," Finn said quietly to the others.

Paul looked toward the building and answered low, "I will hold the back door," and strode off.

They kept watch at the restaurant. Before long a boy brought a note and ran off again.

Paul had scrawled it in haste, Druitt left by the back. I am on him. Will send word.

Finn and Emily finished quickly and took a carriage back to the flat in Mayfair. Later another note arrived by Paul's hand. It held only four words, You were right.

It set the tie among Druitt, Sir Reginald, and the victims in firmer relief.

Chapter Six

Emily's connection with Samuel advanced quickly. Still under the pretext of learning legal work, she met him again. He lent her law books. She read carefully and asked questions when she did not understand. They saw each other often. Each day Emily returned light and bright, as if walking through spring air. Finn was glad for her. The feeling she had for Samuel did not look false.

She did not let feeling blunt her judgment. From Samuel's remarks, she sensed that the senior clerk above him was overly indulgent toward Druitt. Samuel never said it directly, yet the phrasing suggested a private admiration that went beyond ordinary favor. In that age, such attachments could not be spoken. They stayed hidden.

At one in the morning Jessica woke Finn. The London Hospital had sent an urgent note in a hurried hand. O'Leary had been taken.

Finn dressed at once and called for a cab. The wards, usually orderly, were in confusion. A nurse she knew hurried to her, anxious and apologetic. "Miss Parker, I sent for you at once. I had left instructions that no one discharges O'Leary without your consent. The alarm bell rang. The whole place went into an emergency. Someone saw a tall young man with brown hair take O'Leary away. Staff were handling the crisis. No one noticed that he had not been discharged."

"How long?" Finn asked.

"An hour or a little more," the nurse said, looking down.

Finn counted. Near midnight. The hour when attention slackens. Anger would not help. She asked for the man's description, then left at once.

She had no fixed idea where O'Leary had been taken. One place rose first in her mind. His rooms.

The stairwell was dim, with only a few lamps lit behind doors. The air held food and damp. No one watched her. Halfway up, a strong metallic smell met her. Blood. Her chest clenched hard. She opened the door with a small tool.

The blood smell thickened. O'Leary lay dead inside. The throat torn. Fingers severed. Abdomen cut open. Blood spattered the floor. The marks showed torture before death, worked until no more words could be forced out.

Shock and anger rose at once. She bent to examine the body. The warmth had not fully left. The blood was not dry. The skin showed no lividity. The joints were still free. He had been dead about an hour.

A scrap of paper stuck from his sleeve. Finn drew it out with care. In jagged script, You were too late this time. A crude smiling face was sketched at the end.

She searched the room. The killer had been careful. Aside from the blood and the body, the room was as she had

last seen it. No fresh paper. No ink. The note had been prepared in advance and left with intent. She did not linger.

Outside, a cab moved in and out of the fog. The wheels
thumped softly over wet stone. Finn climbed in. Cold mist
soaked her cloak. "Belgravia. Lady Mary's house. Quickly."

As the horse set off, she forced herself to keep the scale
even. She could not let anger fix her on Michael without
proof. Yet O'Leary's body kept returning before her eyes.
The opened belly. The cut fingers. The wet shine of blood.
Three millennia had taught her restraint. They had also taught
her how close justice stands to revenge. She had saved
O'Leary once. She had not stopped his second death. Guilt
gnawed at reason.

If Michael slept quietly in Belgravia, she could strike him
from the list for this night.

At Lady Mary's door she told the driver she would stay
and sent him away. She walked back into the street and took
the fog to Sir Reginald's house.

Michael, as the master's assistant, would not likely be in
the servants' cellar. He would have a room upstairs. Footsteps
neared. Finn slid into the shrubs. The porter made a round,
perhaps drawn by the sound of her cab. When he went back
inside, she waited a few breaths more.

The garden fell quiet. She vaulted to the iron fence, took
the stable roof, and crossed the ridge to a second floor ledge.
Roof tiles quivered underfoot. She kept low.

The first room held a heavy sleeper. The second
breathed even and smelled faintly sweet. The third was too

still. Curtains drawn. No sound of air. Someone lay on the bed, but the chest did not rise. Either the person was dead or the bed was a trick.

Finn pressed a hand to the sash. It gave at once. She slipped in and landed without a sound.

A mound of bedding lay under the cover, shaped to look like a body. "No wonder," Finn murmured. She turned to the rest of the room. The desk held an appointment book filled with Sir Reginald's meetings. The shelves held a few novels and the heavy volumes of reported cases. It was a man's room, an assistant's room, but there were no small personal things.

The wardrobe held neat coats and shirts in Michael's size. She had never seen the master's clerk or secretary. She could not swear it was Michael's room. But someone who built a sleeping decoy had left at night and meant to hide it.

The small places often betray the truth. She checked every pocket. A crumpled bakery handbill. A few pennies. A small stone. A handkerchief.

She opened the handkerchief and held it to her nose. The faint scent of sandalwood. It stirred a thin, near memory she could not yet fix. She took the handbill and the stone and moved back to the sill, set herself in the shadow outside, and waited.

Near dawn, soft steps sounded in the garden. The man pulled a refuse bin under the wall, climbed, pushed aside the vines, and found a rope ladder hidden beneath them. He climbed swiftly from the first to the third floor and crossed to the window. With one motion, he pushed the loose sash inward.

It explained the loosened catch. He had been using the window all along.

Finn saw his face in the weak light. Michael.

Before he could shut the window she moved in and braced it with her hand.

He started, then stepped back.

Finn dropped inside. "You are surprised?" she said.

"It is you, Miss Parker." His pupils widened, then steadied.

"Where have you been."

"That is not your concern."

"The London Hospital. Or the market street."

"I was seeing to private matters. I will not say where."

"Collecting a patient?"

"No," he said, the first word sharp and cold. He tried to smile and only drew the corners of his mouth. The result was something like bravado.

Finn paced once and looked him over. Wet hair. The scent of soap. Short boots.

"You bathe at this hour?" she said.

"I am free to bathe when I wish." His fingers touched his collar.

"Out at night, a stuffed bed to mislead a porter. Suspicious."

"Not as suspicious as a lady climbing into a young man's room at night," he said. "If I call the servants and they find you alone here, it will not look well. I could say I had a late meeting with a young lady. Sir would be annoyed, perhaps, but it is not the same as you being found in my room."

His polite mask had fallen. Finn studied the face beneath.

"How long will you stay," he asked. "I need to sleep." He gestured to the door as if dismissing a caller.

Anger flared. Before he could draw breath she struck precise points at the neck and shoulder. His throat rasped. He could not cry out. Fear crossed his eyes, then that thin edge of pride returned.

"You were right," Finn said quietly. "Call now."

He could not move. He could not speak. A small smear of coal clung to his boot welt. It matched the gritty mud she had lifted from O'Leary's floor. He knew the women introduced by Druitt to Sir Reginald. He moved freely between Belgravia and the East.

If she pressed him here she would bring the house down and lose the line. Justice required evidence, not rage. O'Leary's blood still burned in her sight. She held the line.

She eased him to sit on the bed. With the tip of a knife she loosened the packed grit at his sole, wrapped it in the handkerchief, and met his eyes. "If you have any courage, do not hunt others. Hunt me. I will be waiting. I will find proof."

She stepped back through the window and let the fog close over her.

***

In the morning she took Emily to the cobbler on the corner, Mr. Burns. She showed him the dry mud from O'Leary's floor grooves and the coal dust she had scraped from Michael's boot. He set the samples under a lens. "Fine quartz mixed with coal," he said, voice careful now. "You see this on the south bank by the river. East of London Bridge. Old warehouses. Places near the yards."

They crossed Aldgate and Tower Hill and walked the wharves beneath the bridge. The planks were slick. Coal smoke and river mud came up in the damp. Gaslight stretched the shadows of the warehouse walls. Gangways creaked.

Finn's mind went back to Hanbury Street. The chase had brought her here that night. A figure had slipped like a line of ink through a lane and vanished under a low arch. The sounds had changed at once. The bridge swallowed voices. Only tide and her steps remained.

Emily tugged her sleeve and pointed out fresh and old prints in the grit. This was the place where the line broke that night. The arch and low tunnels gave a clear answer now. He had not vanished. He had gone into the underpass and the cutouts below the bridge. Burns's mix of quartz and coal showed again in the prints.

Someone moved here at night. East of London Bridge. Among the warehouses. The note went into Finn's book.

She pictured a hidden place near the piers. A spot to change clothes, wash, or throw away what could not be taken back to the house. It would leave marks. If they found it, they might take something that spoke plainly.

***

Emily kept seeing Samuel. She had opened a path for him to her uncle's firm. One noon she came into the studio while Finn was finishing a small oil of a Whitechapel street sign.

"It is beautiful," Emily said.

"Thank you," Finn said. "You look happy. Tell me."

"I lunched with my grandparents. Uncle Sir Edward was there. He said the firm will hire Samuel as a clerk. The senior partners like him. He is young and still needs seasoning, but they think he understands process and people, and knows how to handle matters. The senior clerk called him rare. The recommendation on his sheet is from Sir Edward. No one objected." She copied her uncle's laugh with a bright smile.

"That is good news," Finn said. "You and Samuel are getting on. We should have supper with him."

"Yes. I want you to know him," Emily said. "He is not like the men I knew before. Younger than me, but steadier. He gives real counsel. He is respectful."

Finn smiled. Emily was like a younger sister to her. Emily's joy warmed the room.

Finn worked the canvas from memory, giving the buildings their shape. "Faces are easier for me," she said. "Emphasize a few lines and the likeness holds. Buildings are harder to bring out." She showed Emily the portraits.

Emily named what she saw in each face while Finn adjusted small strokes. In Finn's head the route of the chase laid itself out again. He had not known she was above him on the second floor. The path she traced on canvas was the path he had taken.

She painted on. Emily fell quiet. When Finn turned, Emily looked thoughtful, as if something had reached her and then withdrawn.

"Are you well," Finn asked.

Emily nodded. "I will rest a little," she said, and left the room.

Chapter Seven

At dawn, Finn went to the band of riverside warehouses east of London Bridge, tracing one by one the route she had deduced the night before.

Day and night were two different places, the smells of fish, caramel, and coal smoke mixed into a viscous fog; sailors' shouts and laughter crossed and recrossed in the river wind, cranes creaked in the distance, and hawsers and piles were coated with tar and salt mist.

She paused at several archways, the soles of her shoes scraping over boards polished bright by the tide's repeated soaking. In the mud prints lay fine grains of quartz and coal ash, just like the fragment in her memory from last night. After walking a few circuits and seeing it was still early, she decided to visit Annette at the Brown Hotel. She had arranged for Annette to lodge at the Brown Hotel all this time. Near noon she asked at the desk, and the clerk looked up and said, "She has already checked out and settled the bill."

She was taken aback. "Checked out?"

"Yes. Arranged by Miss Ashcroft. She paid the room charge." His tone was calm, and he did not disclose where Annette had gone.

"When was the checkout processed?" she asked.

"Yesterday afternoon."

She gave hurried thanks and immediately hailed a hansom at the door for Hanbury Street. When she arrived, the spare key under the flowerpot outside was gone, and she had no choice but to open the door with her universal pick. The rooms were in disarray, chairs overturned, the tabletop a scatter.

Emily had gone out yesterday afternoon, and Finn had not asked where. They often missed each other's hours. Not seeing her at dawn, Finn had not thought of anything else, yet now, looking at the mess inside, a rush of panic surged up and over. She forced herself to breathe deeply, noted each suspicious point in turn, then called a cab to take her back home at once.

"Jessica, did you see Emily this morning?" she blurted as the maid opened the door.

"No. I went up to tidy her room just now. The bedclothes are exactly as I left them yesterday, so I suppose she didn't come back last night." The maid showed her in as she spoke.

Finn felt the blood drop straight from the crown of her head. She went into Emily's room to check. The bed, as the maid had said, was neat as before. The dressing table was also very orderly, with not a single line left behind. She returned to the study, wrote a letter, sealed it with wax, and instructed Jessica to send a runner at once to Paul's newspaper office, Emily is missing. Annette's lodgings were ransacked. Please first check whether Emily is at your parents' home. I am returning to Annette's residence to wait for you, 146 Hanbury Street. I will ask Samuel whether he met with Emily

She called another cab to the Chambers by London Bridge. As she stepped into the office, a spark flashed through her disorderly mind. She stopped at the door, paid no heed to Samuel seated at the reception desk, and tried to seize that instant of light.

When Samuel saw her he asked, "Miss Parker, are you looking for Druitt?"

She pulled herself together and shook her head. "I'm looking for you. That is to say, I'm looking for Emily. Did you see Emily yesterday?" she asked.

He looked a little surprised, yet still answered, "No. I am to meet her on Saturday."

"She went out yesterday and did not return all night." She paused, weighing how much to reveal.

"She processed the checkout for a friend of ours who was staying at a hotel. I just went to that friend's place and found the rooms in disorder and no one there. I am very worried about her and that friend."

Hearing this, Sameul was at a loss. "Might they be at some other friend's home? It is not so unusual now for them not to come back overnight."

No wonder he did not understand. She truly did not know where to start explaining, so she drew a breath and said, "You are right. I am too anxious. I am very sorry to trouble you. She seldom spends the night out without telling me. If she turns up, could you let me know, or tell her I am looking for her again?" She apologized once more and left.

She hurried to Annette's home. Paul was pacing nearby, his expression tense.

Seeing someone as anxious as she was brought a faint comfort.

"Not at your parents'?" she asked.

He shook his head. She gestured for them to go up together.

"Just so," she said, pointing out the disorder all around, and briefly recounted what she had seen at the hotel and here.

Paul bent to look. "This looks like signs of a struggle."

She nodded. "I find it hard to believe this has nothing to do with Emily or Annette. Only the Ripper does not usually abduct his victims, has he changed his method?"

Paul said nothing. Whether the Ripper abducted women first and then struck, they could not be certain.

At a loss, she suddenly remembered the bakery handbill.

"Let's go to Shad Thames."

They took a cab south, crossed Tower Bridge, and reached the south bank east of London Bridge.

Here a row of red-brick warehouses clung to the river's edge. Damp seeped through the stone joints, and the streets smelled of caramel mingled with fish. Gaslights flickered in the fog, and chains and pulleys chimed softly in the breeze.

On Tooley Street they turned into Bermondsey Wall East, looking for the bakery on the handbill.

She glanced left and right and saw the shop, exactly the one on the flyer.

She stopped and studied the buildings and turns of the alleys.

The warehouse door chains knocked softly in the sea fog, the reek of rust and coal smoke twined and would not disperse. Dark stains of salt damp bled through the red brick, and the smells of fish and caramel rolled and folded in the air.

She stared at the places where shadows layered, as if she could see Emily's afterimage in the broken light.

Paul said in a low voice, "He could not have chosen better. The streets reek of fish and rot. If he dealt with those internal organs here, even if blood flowed out, it would be taken for freshly slaughtered fish. No one would suspect a thing."

His words made her start. There should be the smell of blood here.

She followed him across the slick paving. Scents crossed in the wind. The sharp fish stink should not mask that metallic thread.

But she was not an ordinary person. Having lived for four thousand years, her disciplined breathwork had honed every sense to stillness and edge.

She stilled her thoughts. Somewhere in the quiet, something jarred.

The tip of her tongue tingled, tasting a trace of iron in the air.

She stopped and listened.

The warehouse loomed by the river, doors broad and weathered, an old company mark half erased by time.

Beyond them, nothing. No sound, no draft, yet the silence pressed as if holding its breath.

She stepped closer. The rust scent thickened; faint currents of air stung her skin like fine needles.

Her gaze lifted. High under the roofline, a small vented window caught the gray light, too high for an ordinary climber.

"Try here?" she asked.

Paul hesitated, then gave a short nod.

"Perhaps we should buy a gas lamp," she said quietly. "In case."

They returned with it, the flame small and trembling in the fog. She set her tools to the lock, steady and sure.

When the door yielded, a cold gust burst through and shredded the lamplight into restless shivers.

A narrow beam from the high window struck pilings, scuffed ropes, the warped planks underfoot.

The place breathed of coal and old tidewater, space that could conceal bodies, and where secrets could be quietly moved.

As they stepped in, they saw a great wooden chest lying on its side deeper in.

Her heart was seized by a cold hand. Dark wet marks seeped around the chest, blood and river water mingled and crawled along the seams, like a dark snare that cut that area off into another world.

There was no sound, only a thick halo of light blackening under the lamp. A faint metallic reek hung in the air.

She nearly believed the worst, that she was already gone.

She went forward swiftly. The chest had already been opened. Inside was all blood, thick, black-red, still warm enough to steam in the cold air. Finn's boots stuck to the floorboards with a soft, wet suck. Paul's lamp trembled in his grip. Only then did he speak, voice low and urgent. "Could it be Emily's blood?"

She took the gas lamp from his hand and leaned in. A slat had snagged a bit of cloth. She freed it. Silk. Could it be Emily's garment?

She drew a slow breath and kept her composure. "Let's look around for clues."

Just then, a figure lay curled in the shadows along the wall.

Her heart jumped. She and Paul hurried forward.

It was he, Michael.

His throat had been cut in a sweeping arc, deep enough to show bone. Blood welled like ink, soaking his shirt.

The knife was still in his right hand, the dried blood on the blade consistent with the wound.

"Is he dead?" Paul asked.

She crouched, bringing her nose close to the pool. In the air, the smells of rust and... sandalwood.

She remembered the handkerchief scent in Michael's pocket that night, and the fragrance that had met her that morning at the Chambers, that was the scent on Samuel.

She put on gloves and felt in Michael's pockets, taking out a few coins and a key, then drew a sheet of paper from the inner pocket,

"I can no longer endure any of this. May the Lord have mercy on my soul..., M."

Beneath those prayer-like lines was a list of twenty names and addresses. The handwriting matched exactly that on the anonymous note with the smiling face.

"This is the list of the Ripper's victims and the missing," Paul said.

She nodded.

"This looks... like suicide?" Paul asked.

She measured the wound with her fingers and said softly, "The cut is too clean, too precise. It looks like the work of a surgeon."

He was silent for a moment, then asked, "He is dead. But what about Emily? Did he take her captive?"

She wanted to know that as well. The thought circled at the bottom of her mind.

"Why would Michael die here now? What is the link between him and Emily and Annette's disappearance?" she said. "His death can convince the police the case is over, but we must find the hand behind this performance."

She turned toward the other side of the warehouse, where a few old tables and broken crates stood by the wall. It looked ordinary, like a place where workers lodged temporarily, stocked with daily odds and ends, nothing suspicious.

She paced slowly along the corners, imagining how a killer would hide secrets.

Suddenly she noticed a shadow on the wall out of proportion.

"There seems to be an entrance to an upper level there," she said to Paul. "Let's look for a hanging ladder."

Before long Paul spotted a ladder leaning against the opposite wall.

He carried it quickly to the opening and looked up at her. "Shall we go up?"

She nodded.

He climbed first. The wood underfoot sounded a low note. She followed close behind.

The instant they stepped into the loft, a smell of iron rust mixed with face powder rushed over them.

This was not a simple storeroom, but something like a pathological exhibition hall.

On shelves along the wall lay women's personal effects in neat rows, cheap earrings, broken hairpins, silk handkerchiefs scented with powder, snapped necklaces.

On the other side stood a table laid out with several knives. The edges were dulled and notched, with black flecks lodged in the gaps.

She went to a half-closed wardrobe. Dark workmen's clothes hung within. On the bottom stood several pairs of short boots in a tidy row, the toes scuffed, dusted with mud and ash.

Turning, her gaze fell on a desk by the wall. The wall was plastered with news about the Ripper cases. Stationery and notepaper lay scattered on the desktop.

In the stack of drafts to one side lay a note exactly like the one placed on O'Leary's body, "You were too late this time ☺."

Under the lamp, the smiling face looked feral and grotesque, as if laughing in silence, taunting her.

A weight pressed in her chest. This was his "sanctuary," where he made slaughter into ritual and fixed the victims' afterimages as trophies.

These things were like witnesses for the prosecution, each one staring them down.

She and Paul examined every drawer in the desk. When she pulled the drawer she noticed the proportions were off. Paul drew the whole drawer out and tapped it. There was a second layer inside.

She pried the false bottom carefully. Beneath lay a stack of banknotes. Paul counted them, far beyond what he ought to earn.

She stared at the notes. The money did not belong to the victims, then where had it come from?

Michael had been arranged as a suicide, the list in his breast, the display in the loft, the money in the drawer, all building the same story. Was he a scapegoat? Emily and Annette had been taken from their home; was she laying a trap? Why would she act alone, without consulting her? What made this so hard for her to see? Every question pointed toward the same name, Samuel. She thought of their last conversation before Emily vanished, when she had sat in the studio while Emily stood by the window, studying her portraits.

She had said, "People are easier to draw. Emphasize the features and one can tell at a glance who it is. Buildings are harder, too regular, too without feeling."

Dark brown hair, a square face, a high nose, fair skin, blue eyes,

These features matched Samuel's appearance.

If he and Michael were in league, that would explain everything,

But why would they join hands? Simply because their connections to Druitt and Sir Reginald had brought them together, or was there a deeper design?

Those Whitechapel women's murders, Michael's death, Emily's assault, O'Leary's brutal end, what was hidden behind it all?

She drew a deep breath and steadied herself.

If Samuel truly was involved, he would likely flee now. She shared her suspicions with Paul.

They agreed to notify the police at once and remain in the warehouse to wait for them.

As for her, she had to go back and find Samuel.

✳✳✳

She went to the Chambers intending to ask for Samuel's address. As she stepped inside, he rose to greet her.

"Miss Parker, are you all right? Has Emily come home?" he asked with concern.

She was startled and forced herself to appear calm. "May we sit and talk?" she said.

He was a little surprised, but nodded, settled her in the parlor, and said, "Please wait here. I will find someone to cover the desk for me."

She steadied herself and thought through her approach.

In less than a moment he returned with a cup of hot tea for her.

"Have a sip to settle your nerves," he said gently.

She looked at him. Could it be as they suspected? Was he the Ripper's accomplice?

She decided to test him and told him what they had just found at the warehouse.

"In that wooden chest, a piece of Emily's clothing was left behind."

Samuel went white with shock. "What should we do now? Is there anything I can do?" he asked.

"Think carefully. The last time Emily met you, did she mention anything you found strange?" she said.

"Give me a moment." He rose and walked out.

Soon he returned and handed her a slip of paper.

"After you left this morning, I found this on the desk, pressed under one of my files," he said.

"Annette will return home tonight. I have arranged to meet her with us on Saturday. Emily."

It was Emily's hand, and the tone she used in daily notes. The date was yesterday.

"Who usually receives such messages?" she asked.

Samuel replied, "Usually me. I sit at the front desk. All letters, notes, or court documents delivered to us come first to my hands from the messenger, and I then distribute them to the barristers and clerks. Sometimes, if there is no addressee on the envelope, I leave it on the front table for the person to collect upon return."

He paused, a hint of hesitation in his expression.

She fixed her eyes on him. If he was the one who received the mail, then who had placed this note inside?

"Then why was this note not received by you?" she asked.

Samuel met her gaze, troubled.

"I was just wondering why it did not pass through me," he said. "I went out yesterday on some business. Today I asked the errand boys and other colleagues whether any letters had been delivered while I was away, but they all said in unison that no one had received anything."

His tone was even, with a thread of concern.

"This is very strange," she muttered. "We will report Emily's disappearance to the police. They may come to ask you for details."

"I propose handing this note to the police," Samuel said. "It may help them clarify matters and find her quickly."

"Shall I go back to the warehouse with you now?" he offered.

She looked at him. The doubt in her heart did not disperse. The man in my portrait had borne the same features as Samuel, the dark hair, the fair skin, the square face. And that faint sandalwood scent she had caught on him that morning at the chambers matched both Michael's handkerchief and the odor in the warehouse. Yet perhaps it was all only her conjecture.

Uneasy, she and Samuel took a cab back to the warehouse.

On the way she suddenly realized that the sandalwood fragrance she had smelled on Samuel when she entered the Chambers was gone now.

She frowned. Had he gone home to change?

"Do you live nearby? I am wondering whether Emily might be hiding at your home," she asked.

He started. "I don't think so. She doesn't have my key."

Then he added, "If you wish, we can go by my home first. It is about a mile and a half from here."

He asked the driver to head to Holborn first.

Samuel's lodgings were in a narrow Holborn alley, on the second floor of a three-story old building, a polished number plate hanging at the door.

He opened up for her. Inside, a faint smell of soap and paper hung in the air.

He took her to his room. It was unnaturally neat. A few case files were stacked on the desk, the pen nib still wet with ink. The bed was smooth, nothing amiss.

"I know you and Emily are like sisters," he said gently. "I am worried about her too."

Her eyes burned, and she quickly touched the corners with a handkerchief.

"Could I freshen up a little?" she said softly.

He nodded and led her to a small washroom at the end of the hall.

There was a basin and a mirror there, and a wooden shelf held a few daily items.

She shut the door and made sure the latch had caught. Her gaze swept the room.

On the shelf beside the washstand stood several small glass bottles. She picked one up. Cologne.

She sniffed. It was a different scent.

Then where had the scent she smelled this morning come from?

She drew a deep breath, put the bottle back, and composed herself.

"Let's go to the warehouse now," she said as she stepped out.

***

That afternoon, Inspector Fawson arrived at the scene with his men and immediately sealed off the surrounding area. Officers maintained order as the clerk and coroner soon followed.

Michael's identity was privately disclosed by Paul to the inspector. Fawson was deeply shocked. He ordered that Paul and his newspaper refrain from publishing any details about the warehouse, fearing damage to Sir Reginald's reputation and interference with the investigation.

Paul hesitated, the weight of his editor's expectations clear in his eyes. The paper had already pressed for a lead on the Ripper case, and this was too valuable to lose. Yet he knew when to wait. After a pause, he gave a short nod, allowing the police to speak with the baronet first.

After some bargaining, he agreed to delay the report for three days on one condition, every finding from the inquiry was to reach his office before any other paper. Otherwise, he would publish everything himself at once.

Inspector Fawson, in return, assured him that Emily's disappearance would remain strictly confidential.

Several detectives climbed the narrow stairs to the attic. The light of the gas lamps trembled in the gloom.

The moment they stepped inside, silence fell over the room.

A young constable murmured, "It looks like… an exhibition."

Fawson stared ahead, his voice low and strained. "No. A memorial."

He stood for a moment, grave and wordless, before giving his orders. "Seal the scene. Record everything. Photograph and number each item."

Pens scratched across paper. From one corner came the slow crack of a camera plate being exposed, mingling with the murmurs of men at work. The attic, once orderly and precise, was being methodically dismantled into evidence.

Paul stayed behind to help the police list and sort the exhibits, as well as to give his statement. Finn and Samuel arrived soon after. Samuel handed the inspector a letter.

They watched in silence as officers worked through the warehouse.

"Emily and Annette are both missing," Finn said quietly. "Where could they be?"

Emily had vanished without a trace. Though Paul was deeply troubled, he kept to his duty, writing his report under the agreement that he would not reveal anything about the warehouse or the suspect's death.

By dusk that day, Paul's newspaper was the first to issue an extra edition with the headline, **"Ripper Case, Scotland Yard Discovers Crucial Evidence!"**

The extra had clearly been rushed to print, brief in length yet unusually restrained in tone.

It mentioned no names, no places, and revealed no details.

At the end, Paul added only a single line,

"Sources indicate that the evidence points to an individual connected to the victims' circle. The investigation remains ongoing."

The report caused an uproar across the city.

Within hours, *The Times*, *The Evening Star*, and *The Stand-ard* had reprinted the story, quoting Paul's own phrasing and commentary.

That night, Finn returned to her lodgings. The rain had stopped, but the fog had thickened.

She read Paul's article and the reprints that filled the evening extras.

To drive sales, editors had embellished it with speculative interviews and conjectures.

Reading as a stranger might, Finn searched those vague sentences for the faintest trace that could lead her to Emily.

She could not sleep. Rising from bed, she went into Emily's room, hoping to find a note, a trace, anything to tell her where she had gone, or at least whether the Ripper had taken her.

She searched through notebooks, diaries, clothing, drawers, even the books on the shelves, but found nothing.

As dawn approached, she returned to her own room and sat before the dressing table. In the dim mirror, her tired reflection met her eyes.

Softly, she murmured, "Emily... where are you?"

Chapter Eight

At dawn, the porter, as usual, brought her all the London morning papers.

The front-page headline was even bolder than the evening extra, the letters larger and the tone more emphatic, **"Ripper Case, Scotland Yard Secures Crucial Evidence!"**

Paul's byline lay hidden midway through the article, like an ink stain blurred by rain.

He still abided by the police restriction, mentioning nothing of the warehouse, the attic, or the rope. Instead, he wrote, "Detectives from Scotland Yard have recovered, in a certain East End location, a number of items closely connected to the case. Reliable sources indicate the place had once been briefly occupied by a certain individual. Objects found within correspond closely to the circumstances of the murders. The site has since been sealed."

This piece was clearly longer, and far more polished. He replaced statement with description, skirting the forbidden, yet his words chilled the reader to the core. He wrote of the East End fog, "thicker than usual, as though it meant to swallow the entire alley," and of the woman beyond the police cordon, "a mother holding her child, her eyes as empty as those of a doll." Even without setting foot there, one could almost smell that unnamed place, "coal smoke mixed with decay and cheap gin." He ended with a quiet sting, "Londoners may soon learn the truth, or perhaps they never will." Though the report revealed no location, it stirred the public imagination.

Within a single night, Paul had become the most sought-after crime reporter in London.

Newsboys shouted his name from the street corners, yet no one knew that his real manuscript still lay locked in a drawer, waiting for midnight on the third day.

At noon, just as she finished the thin porridge Karen had prepared, the bell rang.

The maid showed in Paul and Samuel.

"Samuel wanted to see how you were," Paul said.

Samuel looked contrite. "I am very worried about Emily. I thought for a long time last night and realized I spoke without consideration yesterday. I am truly sorry. Paul told me that after you left, no one entered or left Annette's address. I heard you saw signs of a struggle inside. No wonder you are so anxious."

"It is a small matter. Do not think of it," she said.

"But… did the Ripper not already take his own life?" Samuel asked. "Does that mean no one knows where Emily is now?"

Paul looked at her as if asking leave. She nodded.

He considered a moment, then said carefully, "We suspect Michael's death was not a suicide. Either someone executed justice, or the killer silenced him."

Samuel could not hide his surprise.

Paul went on. The marks of Michael's wound did not match self-slaughter. When Samuel heard that all the victims had been Druitt's clients, and that the list found on Michael bore the same names, the color drained from his face.

"Then… is Druitt the real Ripper?" he asked.

"He is the prime suspect, but everything is too conspicuous," Paul said. "We think perhaps the killer hates Druitt, or finds it most convenient to frame him."

Samuel nodded silently, deep in thought.

She added, "We had suspected Michael before, because of his background and some dubious acts. But there was never solid proof. I suspect Emily discovered something. Her disappearance may be tied to the person she suspected." She paused. "To be frank, at the beginning I also suspected you."

Samuel's face changed slightly.

"I am sorry," she said. "You and Michael share certain features, brown hair, fair complexion, regular features, a slender build. And the day I came into the Chambers, I smelled sandalwood on you, exactly the same as on the handkerchief among Michael's clothes." She pointed to two portraits in the parlor. "These I drew from a witness's description."

Samuel stepped closer to study them, as if something had occurred to him, then checked himself.

"I am sorry for that as well," she said with a rueful smile. "Which is why that day I took the chance to go to your home. I found that the cologne you use is not sandalwood."

"It is all right," Samuel exhaled. "At least now you know I am not the killer."

He paused, then asked, "What should we do next?"

She looked to Paul. "Perhaps you can help us clear a few points up. Did Druitt and Michael know each other well?"

"Michael often came to see him, usually to pass messages for Sir Reginald," Samuel said. "They seemed on good terms."

"Did he have enemies?" she pressed.

Samuel thought. "Perhaps clients who lost their cases or could not escape conviction."

She sighed. "That will not be easy to trace."

"Can we get a list of those people?" Paul asked.

"I can try," Samuel said with a nod, then asked, "Do you still think he was framed?"

"Perhaps. But we cannot rule him out either. Every lead points to him," she said.

They were silent for a time.

Finn looked at the newspapers on the table and said to Paul, "You're now the most sought-after reporter in London. Emily would be proud of you."

A flicker of restrained anger crossed his proud expression.

"If it weren't for Scotland Yard's order to postpone the details for three days, the whole city would have gone mad by now," he said quietly, his voice steady yet edged with frustration.

He took a bundle of papers from his briefcase, his movements cautious and deliberate.

"This will be published in two days."

He handed her the manuscript for review.

Paul described what he had witnessed at the scene with remarkable clarity. His eye for detail was extraordinary, his account of the warehouse was so vivid that even without setting foot there, the reader could feel the chill from his depiction of the loft.

The article made no accusation of police negligence; its tone remained measured.

He had deliberately omitted the mention of the banknotes in the drawer, as well as Michael's name and his connection to Sir Reginald.

"You write not only with precision but with depth," Finn said sincerely. "You've managed to make every detail of the warehouse come alive without a hint of excess, gripping and impossible to put down. A report like this is bound to cause a greater stir. No wonder Emily admired you so deeply."

She pointed to the box beside her and added softly, "These are her clippings. She kept every one of your articles."

Paul had once written on daily life and current affairs, only moving to breaking news two years ago.

A complicated look passed over Paul's face.

"We will find Emily," Samuel said, breaking the silence.

Paul seemed to remember something. "You said yester-day we should meet Sir Reginald and trace the source of the five hundred pounds. I have asked Inspector Fawson to arrange it. I will go to see him this afternoon."

Seeing Samuel's confusion, he added, "We found five hundred pounds in cash hidden in a secret compartment in the warehouse."

Samuel gave a low whistle. "That is no small sum."

"It does not match his income," she said. "Perhaps Sir Reginald can explain it. Are you going to him as a reporter?"

"Yes," Paul said. "I plan to request an interview, write a piece on him, and put him at ease."

She nodded. Meeting Sir Reginald herself would have to wait.

Paul checked his watch, then rose to take his leave.

Paul went on to Belgravia. Samuel stayed with her. She asked if he had wanted to tell them something earlier. He hesitated.

She reminded him, "When we spoke of Druitt just now, you seemed to have something to say."

He was silent for a moment, then said, "I do not wish to cause unnecessary misunderstanding."

"We all want Emily home safe," she said. "Finding the Ripper's confederate is our only way forward. Any information may help."

He looked out at the street. After a long moment he said in a low voice, "You mentioned the sandalwood. I did spray some sandalwood cologne at my station. Druitt gave it to me a month ago. He said it was a brand he liked, and since the shop was running a special, he bought an extra bottle. He said it was to thank me for handling his documents." He gave a strained smile. "In truth, handling documents is my job."

He paused, then added, "A week ago he asked why I was not using the cologne he gave me, so now every morning I spray a little at my seat."

He looked up at her. "And as for brown hair, fair complexion, regular features, a slender build, perhaps I have seen Druitt so often that the image that rises in my mind is always his."

She started, then nodded. Druitt was a little older, and their attention had been fixed on Matthew, the younger man in his twenties, so they had never looked closely enough to notice how alike the features were.

"I am not saying Druitt is a suspect," Samuel went on. "I have always respected him. He is an excellent barrister. I only mean these descriptions could fit many people. At least you have already identified Michael correctly."

"But if he truly was connected to those victims, and several of his clients also disappeared from Whitechapel, does that not raise his suspicion further?" he asked.

"Perhaps he is clever enough to use a counter-plot to shield himself," she said.

"Druitt graduated with first-class honors from Oxford," Samuel added. "I did not understand what that meant before. Later the senior clerk told me that anyone who leaves such a place with top marks is unquestionably intelligent."

They fell into a long silence.

"What do we do now?" Samuel asked at last.

"The police have already ruled the Ripper case closed," she said. "So we have only ourselves to continue the investigation."

After a while she asked Samuel to tell her everything he knew about Druitt and the Chambers.

Samuel left at dusk. The house settled back into its chill. Without Emily, the rooms felt especially hollow. She took out her earlier notes and compared them, one by one, with what Samuel had said.

She had just pried out of Samuel the Chambers' working hours and guard arrangements, which gave her an idea. That night, she decided to slip into Druitt's office. By day the place teemed with people; at night the porter locked up and made his rounds. The barristers usually left before ten, so she chose to act after that.

That night the whole set of offices was unusually quiet, the stone steps answering only her own tread. Timing her move for when the porter on rounds had gone farther down, she slipped into Druitt's rooms by the side door.

As she pushed the door, a thread of sandalwood lingered inside, faint and almost fading, yet recognizable.

The room was immaculate. Files were stacked in order. Even the pen nibs had been polished to a shine. The excessive tidiness sharpened her unease.

She searched between desk and cabinet for a long time and at last found, in the inner layer of a file, half a torn sheet.

The hand was hurried and familiar. It was a draft of a black-mail letter he had not managed to destroy. The lines breathed cold calculation. Her chest tightened until she could hear her heartbeat echo in the still room.

***

The air in the study was close, the fire in the grate a weak glow.

Sir Reginald looked far older than before, yet a kind of anxious hunger flickered in his eyes, a hunger to be understood.

When he spoke, his voice was hoarse and urgent. "That boy… I never imagined he would be involved in such crimes. He seemed so upright."

Paul listened without comment, noting only a few lines in his book.

Sir Reginald went on. "He always trusted him greatly."

He paused, lifted his gaze to Paul, and spoke in a low tone. "I know his background would be exposed one day. I only want the world to understand that I have always provided education and many opportunities for him and for the poor of Whitechapel. I do not wish Michael's matter to turn good deeds into disaster. That would make it even harder for anyone to extend a helping hand in future. And I, too, am a victim."

Paul nodded. "Your service to Whitechapel is evident. I can frame you as a victim, and one who will continue to give to the poor."

At this Sir Reginald brightened, nodding vigorously, his earlier dejection swept aside.

Paul's tone shifted. "But you must speak frankly about certain matters concerning you and the Ripper's victims."

Sir Reginald's face changed as he weighed his position.

"It is better you tell me everything," Paul said, "than that another reporter bring these findings to light. And I may not report every detail. There was a list of victims on Michael. I will publish that. What I will not say is that the people on the list had all worked in your household. And that the certified victims had, with you, a relationship that was not entirely ordinary."

At this, Sir Reginald went ashen.

"Tell me first what you know concerning Michael," Paul said calmly. "Did you allow Michael to approach those women with whom you had that not-entirely-ordinary involvement?"

Paul's calm brought Sir Reginald to calm as well. "Whom I met day to day, Michael knew almost to a one. After Druitt made the introductions, he handled most engagements. So he was by no means unconnected with those who were later killed."

Suddenly his expression changed as if something had clicked. "It all makes sense. Those anonymous letters were plainly his own play. I even thanked him for helping me deliver the hush money. Second bench by the path in Hyde Park, the rubbish bin at its side; third box in the second row at the General Post Office… hm. All positions of his arranging."

Thinking of the stack of notes in the drawer, Paul looked up. "You mean he sent the anonymous demands, and you had him pass on the hush money?"

Sir Reginald clenched his jaw. "Yes. Only now do I see it. The very man I handed the money to was the blackmailer."

"Did you keep the letters?" Paul asked.

Sir Reginald stopped, weighed the risk, then sighed. "Better in your hands than someone else's." He rose, opened a drawer, and handed Paul a thick stack. "The letters kept coming. At first only ten pounds. I did not mind it then, thinking it would spare a scandal. After I had paid about two hundred, I did not want to give more and thought the other side would not dare press further. It was not a great sum and did not seem to warrant going to the police. Then, six months ago, the Ripper appeared. The letters began to hint that I was involved, and that each victim was connected to me. The price leapt to two hundred pounds each time. I was to seal the cash and give it to Michael, who would place it where instructed. Every time there was another murder in the streets, I received a letter the next day. Counting it all, I have paid one thousand pounds in hush money. I did not dare refuse. If anyone suspected I had a hand in the case, my name would be ruined."

Paul read as he listened. The sums demanded were bold indeed. Even for Sir Reginald's means, it could not go on forever.

"So you kept paying?" Paul asked.

"What else could I do? Report it? If the police suspected me, the whole family would be dragged down."

Paul remembered the cash in the drawer. It was far short of that total. Could it be that Sir Reginald had realized Michael was the blackmailer, had someone kill him in the warehouse, and recovered the money? The thought flickered, then he dismissed it. If Sir Reginald were behind it, he would likely have erased every trace. No one would know of these accounts.

He closed his notebook and spoke evenly. "I will consider how to write this. I do not wish to deprive those in Whitechapel who need help of your donations."

"I leave it to you," Sir Reginald said.

Chapter Nine

It was the third day of Emily's disappearance.

At noon she received a note from Paul inviting her to meet at a tea shop near the Chambers.

While they waited for Samuel, she drew out a clipping.

"Paul, I found this among Emily's keepsakes," she said, spreading the yellowed paper on the table.

It was a feature he had written three years earlier for his press, *"The Underground World of London."*

In it, he had described the city's labyrinth of conduits and the unseen life that stirred beneath its streets.

> *"By 1888, the principal sewer system of London was still under the charge of the Metropolitan Board of Works, engineered in the mid-nineteenth century by Mr. Joseph Bazalgette to carry the waste waters downstream. The trunk lines extended along both banks of the Thames, carefully maintained by the authorities and closed to the general public.*
> *Beneath and about them, however, there endured fragments of older channels and branches,*

relics of an age preceding the great works of the century. Some had fallen into decay; others were adapted to new uses.

In the East End and the docklands, such disused culverts were said to lead toward breweries, warehouses, and the riverfront. Certain merchants and laborers availed themselves of these forgotten ways for the conveyance of goods, or as vaults for coal and barrels of fish. Others turned them into cold-rooms or temporary stores. Owing to their antiquity, many of these passages were absent from official maps, their mouths hidden among cellars and embankments, known only to those long acquainted with the ground."

"Around Fleet Street and Whitechapel, traces of former streams and old drainpipes could still be seen, with brick vaults and a clammy smell. Certain sections were closed in name only yet remained passable, becoming private underground routes for the few."

He looked at the article and gave a slightly uneasy smile. "Ah, that article."

"I read the whole night," she said. "I did not know there were so many passages beneath our feet. I am wondering if the Ripper used these conduits, which is why he could evade pursuit."

She also remembered the night she had lost the knife-man mid-chase. Perhaps that was where he vanished.

Paul thought about it, his tone pausing. "That was three years ago. Let me think."

After a moment's reflection he said, "I did some research then. People who knew the area took me into one or two of the conduits that could still be entered. But as far as I know, some passages have long been out of repair or turned to other uses."

"So it is possible the Ripper used them?" she asked.

Paul hesitated, then nodded.

At that moment Samuel entered the tea shop.

After greetings, Paul told them in outline what he had discussed with Sir Reginald the day before.

"So the Ripper's motive was money?" Samuel asked.

"Perhaps, and the pleasure of killing," she said coolly.

Samuel stirred his tea absently. "By the way, Druitt didn't come to chambers today. No word sent either."

Her heart tightened. "Does he often fail to appear?"

Samuel shook his head. "Never. If he will be out, he always informs us in advance."

The alarm sounded in her mind at once.

She looked at Paul. He sensed, as she did, that something was wrong.

"Can you look into Druitt's office to see if anything stands out?" Paul asked Samuel.

"I will go with Finn to his house," he said, glancing at her.

She nodded. They left the shop at once and took a cab toward Blackheath.

The porter knew her. She handed over five shillings, and he opened the door for them.

"I will wait here for him. Pay us no mind," she said, to give a reason for letting them in.

He understood, gave a knowing smile, and withdrew, closing the door.

Inside, the curtains were half drawn. The place bore the marks of hasty tidying. The wardrobe had been cleared, and many of the toiletries in the small washroom were gone. A faint trace of sandalwood lingered.

They searched the house carefully. Apart from the signs of clearing out, there was nothing to indicate where Druitt had gone.

"Did he disappear of his own will, or is he a victim of the Ripper as well?" Paul said. "Or perhaps he is the one who killed Michael and took Emily, and now he is using the chance to flee."

One question followed another. None could be answered.

They returned to the Chambers and waited for Samuel in the same tea shop.

"Anything?" she asked.

Samuel produced the half-torn blackmail letter she had left the previous night.

"It is him," Paul said. "To obtain more money, Druitt posted the letter to the paper. This matches exactly what Sir Reginald described."

"I knew he was pressed and had to make do on teaching and referral fees, but I never imagined he would… kill for money," Samuel said, his voice shaking.

"Then why did he kill Michael?" she asked.

"He wanted the police to close the case so he could walk away," Paul said.

"If he has vanished, the chance of finding Emily will be even smaller," she said.

After a pause she added, "We should search the underground conduits."

After some discussion they decided to start from the warehouse. She would go to the library to find plans of the conduits, and Paul would return to the paper to consult his old columns.

To avoid attention, they chose to return to the warehouse at midnight.

Chapter Ten

The police cordon still hung across the door, its twine fixed to the bolt with sealing wax. Finn took out her pick and gently worked the latch free. The metallic click was small in the quiet street.

The air inside was stagnant, heavy with damp and the must of old wood. The police had left their forensic kit behind. Dusted patches, labeled slips, and upturned boxes remained on the floor. Aside from these new traces, the warehouse was almost as they had left it.

They lit the gas lamps. Orange light threw wavering shadows on the walls. This area had been, decades earlier, an entry to the riverside conduits. Many cellars and drains had later been sealed or converted to private uses.

They were looking for the secret way to the old channel. Paul walked with the lamp, inspecting the corners. The walls wept moisture, and there was the faint sound of water under the floor.

Suddenly he called in a low voice, "Here."

Finn and Samuel went to him at once. Paul pushed aside a half-closed crate. Beneath it, a rusted iron ring was exposed.

"It looks like the mouth of an old ventilator shaft," Paul said.

Finn knelt and ran a finger across it. "No dust, no cobwebs," she said. It had seen use recently. The cover was heavy. The ring had nearly fused with the floor.

Paul found an iron hook and a short bar in the warehouse. He and Samuel pried together. The iron ring didn't groan; it shrieked. They heaved the cover aside.

Below them, a square of absolute blackness swallowed the light of their lanterns. The air that rose from the shaft was a physical blow, a humid, heavy rot that smelled of ancient mud and the iron tang of the river.

"I go first," Finn said. Her voice sounded small against the stone.

She descended the rusted rungs. Her boots slipped on the slime. She did not use her disciplined breathwork to remain calm; she used it because the air was too thin to breathe otherwise. At the bottom, the conduit stretched away in a low, vaulted arch of dripping brick. They moved in silence for a mile. The only sound was the rhythmic clack-clack of the water dripping from the ceiling and the distant, low thrum of the Thames above them.

Then, the light hit it. Three hundred paces ahead, a shape was lashed to a support pillar. It was white silk, a woman's form.

"Emily!" Paul cried, his voice echoing like a gunshot. He started to run.

"Wait!" Finn caught his arm, but he wrenched away.

She felt it before she saw it. There was a shift in the air. She heard the snick of a hammer falling. There was only a flash of orange in the dark, then a roar. The lead ball shattered the brick inches from her head, spraying her with red dust and grit. It was a flintlock pistol rigged to a tripwire.

"Stay down!" Finn hissed, lunging for the shadow near the pillar.

But the light from the dropped lantern showed the truth. The figure tied to the pillar was not Emily; it was a decoy draped in her dress. Finn turned, her senses screaming. Behind her, Paul was not cowering. He was standing perfectly still, the light of the remaining lantern carving deep, hollow shadows into his face. He looked different without his spectacles. He looked like the man in Finn's portrait. He looked like a monster.

He held a pistol, leveled at her chest.

"You really do have a nose for the truth, Finn," Paul said. His voice was no longer tired. It was melodic. "But the truth in Whitechapel is usually buried under six feet of muck."

"You used her," Finn felt her heart hammering against her ribs. It was a fast, rhythmic thud. It was a sensation of vulnerability she had not felt in centuries. "Your own niece."

"A means to an end," Samuel's voice drifted from a side arch. He stepped into the light, a surgical scalpel glinting between his fingers. "She saw the portrait, Finn. She saw Paul's face in your sketches. She was too clever for her own good. Just like you."

Finn tried to move, to use the speed she had spent four thousand years perfecting, but the air here was a trap of its own. Her boots were deep in the silt. Paul did not wait. He pulled the trigger.

The pain was not a burning tear. It was a white-hot sledgehammer that took her breath and her legs. The bullet caught her in the shoulder, spinning her back into the freezing, rising water of the conduit.

"The tide is coming in, Finn," Paul said. His voice faded as they backed toward the ladder. "In five minutes, this sanctuary will be filled to the ceiling. You can spend eternity here. It is a quiet place for a legend to die."

Finn lay in the mud, the water already lapping at her chin. Her blood was black in the lantern light. For the first time in a millennium, she did not feel like a legend. She felt cold.

The darkness pressed in, thick with the sound of her own ragged breathing and the relentless slosh of the rising river. The Thames did not just rise; it inhaled, pushing a wall of icy, brackish water deeper into the brick veins of the city. The bone in her shoulder grated like broken porcelain. Finn reached up with her good hand, her fingers trembling as she sought the nerve cluster near her collarbone. She dug her thumb in, hard. A jolt of electric agony sparked through her vision, followed by a merciful, heavy numbness. She could not fix the hole, but she could silence the scream of the flesh.

Finn forced herself upright. The silt at the bottom of the conduit was like wet cement, dragging at her skirts. The water was at her waist now, swirling with the refuse of a million lives above. Paul and Samuel were gone, the distant thud of the iron cover sealing the shaft echoing like a coffin lid being nailed shut.

Four thousand years of survival, and it came down to a drowned tunnel in a city that had not existed when she was born. Finn looked at the decoy, the wooden frame draped in Emily's white silk. It bobbed mockingly in the rising tide. Her lantern was gone, but a faint, ghostly luminescence clung to the walls, phosphorescence from the sewer's decay.

Then she saw it. Near the support pillar where the decoy hung, the water was not swirling; it was being sucked inward. There was a steady, rhythmic gulping. She waded toward it, her boots heavy as lead. Behind the pillar, half submerged in the rising flood, was a secondary sluice gate, an old wooden door reinforced with iron. It was locked from this side with a heavy crossbar.

But it was the scrap of fabric caught in the iron hinge that caught her breath. It was a fragment of a dark wool shawl.

Emily's shawl. She was not dead. Samuel had not brought her here to kill her. He had brought her here to hide her. He wanted Finn to see the decoy and be shot by Paul. He wanted her to drown in despair while Emily sat inches away.

The girl was trapped in a pocket of air behind the sluice gate. It was a game of cruelty. It was a signature Finn recognized. The malice was familiar. It was the work of a shadow from a dead world.

"Emily!" Finn croaked. The water reached her chest. A muffled thud came from the other side of the wood, a frantic, rhythmic kicking.

"I'm here!" Finn shouted, the salt water splashing into her mouth. She threw her weight against the iron crossbar. It did not budge. Her numb left arm was a dead weight, useless. She braced her feet against the support pillar and used her good shoulder, shoving until the skin tore and the iron bit into her collarbone.

She let the tide rise until it reached her chin. She took one last, deep lungful of the foul air and submerged. Under the water, the world was a blur of brown and grey. She found the crossbar again. With the buoyancy of the water lifting her, she put both feet against the stone wall and pulled with every ounce of her ancient soul. The wood groaned. The bar snapped with a sound like a bone breaking.

The door swung inward with violent force. The rushing water swept Finn through the opening like a leaf in a storm. She tumbled into a small, dry stone alcove, a maintenance crawlspace that sat just above the lower drain's level. She landed hard on her wounded side, a fresh wave of blackness threatening to take her.

A small, cold hand caught hers. "Finn?"

Emily was huddled in the corner, her face a mask of soot and tears. She was shivering violently, but her eyes were wide and sharp.

"It is my uncle," Emily said. The words were a thin, jagged whisper.

"I know," Finn whispered, pulling the girl into her good arm. "I know everything."

Finn looked at her blood-soaked shoulder, then up at the ceiling where the water was still thundering against the door. A faint draft of fresh air was blowing in from a ventilation grate. It smelled of fog and carriage horse exhaust. Mayfair was miles away, but for the first time in three days, Finn could smell the surface.

"Can you walk?" Finn asked.

Emily stood up, swaying, and wiped the grime from her face. Her fear was there, but beneath it was something new, a cold, quiet rage.

"I can run," Emily said.

"Good," Finn replied, tearing a strip from her hem to tie a makeshift sling. "Because we have a funeral to arrange. And I need Paul to be the guest of honor."

***

The cold air of the wharves was a shock to her lungs. Finn and Emily collapsed onto the slick cobbles of Shad Thames, hidden between two towering warehouses. They could hear the city beginning to stir, the early morning calls of the mudlarks and the distant rattle of the milk carts.

"Finn, your arm," Emily whispered, her voice trembling.

"I will survive. I always have." Finn leaned against a damp brick wall, watching the fog roll off the Thames. "But your uncle won't. Not when he realizes his ideal partner has been playing a different game entirely."

Finn knew Samuel's signature now. Paul was a fool who thought he was the director of this play, but he was merely the lead actor. Samuel was the one who had built the stage. Samuel did not care about the fame of being the Ripper; he cared about the slow breaking of a human soul, the way he could mold the dark side of a man like Paul into a weapon. He wanted to watch how humanity slides from the light into the dark.

"We can't go to the police," Emily said. "He has the papers. He is the most sought after reporter in London."

"I don't need the police," Finn said, the numbness in her shoulder beginning to fade into a dull, throbbing heat. "I need Paul to feel the one thing he can't handle, the fear of being forgotten."

They did not go back to Mayfair. Finn took Emily to the small, quiet inn near Blackheath where she had hidden the real Montague John Druitt. The barrister was a broken man, hiding in the shadows of a tiny room, terrified that the world would soon brand him a monster. Finn spent the next twenty-four hours in a fever of movement. She sent Emily to Lady Mary's house to hide under her protection. Meanwhile, Finn tracked the sandalwood scent one last time.

It led back to the river. Samuel had done exactly what Finn expected. Once the play was over and the protagonist was supposedly dead, the tool became a liability.

Finn found Paul Ashworth's body downstream at midnight. Paul did not die like a legend. There was no surgical precision on his body, no signature marks of the Ripper's blade. Instead, he lay soaked and silent, his lungs heavy with the river's silt, a death that the papers would easily call a desperate suicide by drowning. His eyes were still open, fixed in a stare of pure, human disbelief. He had died realizing that he was not the monster; he was just the monster's dinner.

Samuel was nowhere to be seen, but the air still held that faint, mocking scent of sandalwood. Finn looked down at Paul's body. To the world, he was a hero journalist. If his body was found here as he was, the investigation would continue. Samuel would simply find a new tool.

"You wanted to be remembered, Paul," Finn whispered, reaching into her bag. "I am going to make sure you are. But not as yourself."

She took Druitt's dark wool overcoat, which she had taken from the inn. She pulled the silver watch, engraved with M.J.D., from her pocket. Finn began the grim work of dressing the dead journalist in the barrister's life. With the murders having finally ceased, a body found under such circumstances would provide the silent conclusion the authorities craved. The city would find its peace, and the investigation would eventually fade into the fog.

Finn finished dressing the body and dragged it toward the exit that led to the river slipway. It was heavy, the weight of a man's failed ambitions. She watched until the dark wool was swallowed by the black water.

A week later, Finn sat in the Mayfair parlor with Emily. The morning papers were spread across the table. The Times carried the item, "The barrister Montague John Druitt is believed to have taken his own life by drowning, owing to mental distress."

Emily looked at Finn, her face pale but steady. "Is it over, Finn?"

"The murders have stopped," Finn said softly.

After a long silence Emily asked, "What about Samuel?"

The mist crept in again. Whenever Samuel was mentioned, the fog arrived as if it remembered what was unfinished.

Finn remembered the letter that had arrived a few days earlier.

***

"Dear Miss Parker,

You do not like mysteries. Neither do I. I thought about it for a long time. When I saw the recent news, I understood. You took Druitt away, did you not? Rest easy. I will not look for him. This affair is finished. I suppose what you care about more is how I met Paul.

From the first moment I saw him, I knew he would be an ideal partner. A warped mind, convinced of insult, hungry for success. That quality that burns on grievance, I see it at a glance, and I use it best. We got on well. Perfect cooperation, mutual need. Everything was perfect. No one suspected. Until the day he mentioned you.

He said you were investigating the Ripper case. I did not think much of it at first, but from that moment, everything became much more interesting. We met again. Not the first time, and not the last. On a certain night centuries ago, in a fortress in the north of France, you looked at me the same way. The fire, the judgment, and that addictive fear. After that night, we both thought the other was gone.

"Mais le temps finit toujours par faire revenir les vieilles choses."

You pursue the light, and I watch how it collapses. You spend a life hunting truth, and I like to watch how people slide from the light into the dark. This time, let us call it a draw. Time is long, and I have patience. Perhaps one night, when the fog climbs your window again, I will stand at the foot of your bed and watch you sleep in silence. Will you dream of me, or will you wake, and in that instant feel a joy at our reunion?

We will meet again.

Samuel"

Emily's voice was barely above a whisper. "Do you think he is still alive?"

Finn looked toward the window. In her mind flickered the image of that boy, burned and buried across the ruins of castles in France more than a century ago. The morning mist was lifting. Sunlight touched the corner of the newspaper on the table.

"Yes," Finn said softly. "And he always will be."

She touched her shoulder, where the scar would forever remain, a reminder that even legends can bleed.

The next time the fog rose, she would not be hunting a ghost named the Ripper. She would be hunting the man who had given him the knife.

Afterword

Annette had returned home, eager to show them the places she thought worth visiting. Whitechapel, now that no new victims of the Ripper had appeared, seemed oddly alive again. When they passed Spitalfields Market, Finn noticed the barman behind the counter.

It was one of the few mysteries she had yet to untangle. She stepped into the bar and greeted him.

He squinted at her, then broke into a wide grin. "Well, look at you! Dressed like a fine lady today." He pointed playfully at her clothes.

Finn smiled and ordered a pint, then asked about the night he had failed to meet her.

"I wanted to come, easy money and all that," he said, rubbing the back of his neck, "but on my way home I felt someone following me. I remembered poor O'Leary getting himself hurt and ending up in hospital. Thought maybe it had something to do with that gentleman and young Matthew I saw on Dorset Street. The more I thought about it, the more frightened I got. That day he ran into Matthew at the market, and then, well, you know what happened after." He sighed. "Luckily, I bumped into a group of workers heading to a building site. I joined them and never went home. I took the two pounds you gave me and bought a passage back to my homeland. When I heard the Ripper had taken his own life, I came straight back. Wanted to say a proper goodbye to O'Leary."

He looked down, his expression heavy with sorrow.

Finn was silent for a while before she asked, "So you always knew about Matthew?"

"Aye," he said. "O'Leary told me everything. I knew the lad well, I've been around this neighborhood all my life."

He scratched his head thoughtfully.

If he hadn't left London that night, Finn thought, perhaps their investigation might have reached the truth sooner. O'Leary had been tortured maybe the killers believed he knew where the barman had gone. Those were things she would never know.

She was simply grateful the barman had survived.

Finn finished her beer quietly, then placed five Pounds on the counter. "That's for the information," she said.

He laughed heartily.

In London's fog, some mysteries never cleared, but some people, somehow, still found a glimmer of light.

The End

The Nordholm Mystery: 2026

After the case involving the two detectives murdered at the abandoned construction site was closed, more than a month passed without Finn seeing Leon Chase.

A few days ago, he had sent her a brief message saying he had taken on a new case. He did not elaborate, but they agreed to meet in person to discuss the details.

That afternoon, Finn sat in her favorite coffee shop in downtown Nordholm, sipping her coffee as she waited for Leon to arrive. The café's front was all glass. As she drank, she watched the steady flow of pedestrians outside, people moving past one another with practiced indifference.

The scene outside drifted through her mind without leaving an impression. Then, without warning, her skin prickled. For a moment, she thought she recognized an old acquaintance. Finn leaned forward and looked again, but the figure was already gone, swallowed by the busy street.

His appearance here was not, in itself, unusual. But during their last conversation, he would have known she was in Nordholm. If he had come to this city, why had he not contacted her?

She caught the eye of a familiar barista and gestured toward the door. The woman nodded. Finn turned, opened the door, and walked in the direction where she had last seen him. She knew these streets well. As she walked, she scanned the shops on both sides, letting her gaze move without haste. After more than twenty minutes, she found nothing.

"Maybe I was mistaken," she murmured. She shook her head and turned back, once again searching the storefronts as she retraced her steps.

When she returned to the café, Leon still had not arrived. She sat back in her earlier seat and picked up her phone. She typed a message and sent it, *"I just saw someone who looks a lot like you. I even chased after them. I thought it might be a surprise."*

Leon's office was no more than a ten-minute walk from the café, yet there was nothing. No updates. No explanation. Finn waited for over half an hour. She sent another message. No response. She called him; it rang until the system cut the connection.

At that point, waiting no longer made sense.

Finn left the café and went straight to his office. The elevator carried her to the top floor, the director's level. The receptionist, Angel, greeted her but confirmed Leon was not in. Finn asked to see his assistant, Rachel. When Rachel saw her, she looked up in surprise.

Rachel explained that Leon had left the office at 3:00 p.m. that afternoon. Before leaving, he had said he was meeting Finn at 3:30 p.m. Finn checked the time. It was already 4:30 p.m.

Leon Chase had vanished.

Rachel began calling his driver. "You said he told you he would go to the café by himself, right?" Finn reminded her.

Rachel nodded, her hands trembling slightly as she called the driver. The answer was no. The driver had not seen Leon at all that afternoon. Rachel tried Leon's phone again. Still no answer. She moved to her computer and brought up the internal tracking system. The locator icon hovered within the building.

They exchanged a brief look. "Can you check whether he actually left the building?" Finn asked.

Rachel immediately called the security supervisor. They confirmed that Leon had exited the building about an hour earlier. He was officially out of contact. As the head of the Chase Group, his disappearance was not just a personal matter. It was a corporate catastrophe. Rachel's composure was fracturing, but her training took over. She notified the group's security chief and the COO, initiating the highest-level crisis response.

"But the tracker is still inside the building," Rachel murmured. She typed a few more commands. "The signal is coming from the 12th floor. They are sending a team now."

"I am going with them," Finn said.

They took the elevator to the 12th floor, the customer service hub. As they descended, Finn asked if Leon ever went off the grid. Rachel's answer was a firm no.

The elevator doors opened to a vast space of glass and shadows. Rachel swiped her card to enter the secure zone.

Finn kept her eyes sharp. She looked for anything out of place. And then she saw it. On a desk in the center of the room sat Leon's phone. It was placed perfectly straight, as if on display.

Finn stepped past the security team. The wooden box lay beneath the phone, looking weathered and out of place in the glass office. She felt the energy radiating from the wood. It was the weight of 1888.

Finn felt a cold surge of adrenaline. She knew this box. A heavy, sweet scent drifted from the grain, mixed with the metallic tang of old dust and dried blood. It was sandalwood.

She lifted the lid. Inside, resting on a bed of velvet, was a silver ring. It was a woman's ring, tarnished by a century of time. The silver still carried that distinct, haunting aroma.

Emily's ring.

Finn's breath hitched. She had thought the trophies taken by Paul and Samuel were lost. She had thought they were destroyed in a warehouse fire decades ago. But Samuel did not destroy things. He kept them. The belongings of the dead were stakes in a game that never ended.

She looked toward the window. Her mind went back to the acquaintance she had seen on the street. It had not been a stranger. It was Wayne.

If Wayne was here in Nordholm and had not told her, it meant only one thing. Samuel was not just watching from the shadows anymore. He was moving the pieces.

Leon Chase was the first pawn to fall.

The Legend Continues

Finn Parker will return in **Legend: The Nordholm Mystery: 2026**.

The game has moved from the fog of 1888 to the steel of Nordholm. The puppeteer has revealed his face. The hunt is no longer a memory.

The past is coming for the present.

Coming in 2026.

Historical Note

In 1888, London lived with fear. The violence was real, and many questions were never answered. The White-chapel murders happened, the panic they caused was absolute, and the fog hung thick over the city, dimming lamps and swallowing entire streets.

Whitechapel and Spitalfields formed a crowded labyrinth of rookeries and narrow courts where seventy thousand people were packed into a few square miles. Spitalfields Market was the heart of the district, a place of noise, rotting produce, and desperate trade. Many streets were so narrow that sunlight rarely reached the cobblestones. Poverty in the East End was nearly impossible to escape, and the "Penny Sit-up" and the "Four-penny Lean-to" were the only beds many could afford.

Characters like O'Leary reflect the Irish immigration of the period. Thousands fled famine and poverty in Ireland to find work on the London docks, and they often faced deep prejudice in the city. For the working class, the local bar or "gin palace" was the only public space they could claim. It was a place of heat and light in a city that offered little of either. The local hospitals and churches, like Christ Church Spitalfields, stood nearby, offering what support they could.

History generally agrees on the five women known as the Canonical Five, all murdered in the autumn of 1888. They were real women, mothers, widows, and daughters, who had struggled against poverty and hardship in Whitechapel. Most of them worked long hours at washing, mending, or casual labor just to survive, yet society offered them almost no protection or safety net.

Beneath the streets of London, another world was quietly taking shape. The expanding sewer system built by Joseph Bazalgette, together with the new underground railways, created a network of tunnels and passages. In places these hidden corridors ran dark and forgotten, offering routes where a person could move unseen from one part of the city to another.

In contrast, the West End districts of Mayfair and Belgravia were centers of power, with wide avenues and quiet mansions. Brown's Hotel, founded in 1837, remains a real landmark of this world, serving the elite and foreign visitors to the capital.

In this world, men like Sir Reginald Whitmore truly held the reins of power. A high-ranking adviser in the Home Office, he moved through the hushed drawing rooms of Belgravia and the marble halls of Whitehall, where decisions that shaped thousands of lives were made with little public scrutiny.

The actual practice of the law belonged to barristers such as Montague John Druitt, men in wigs and black gowns who argued their cases in the ancient chambers of the Inns of Court. Between these two poles of influence lay Fleet Street, noisy and ink-stained, where journalists like Paul Ashworth turned the city's darkest events into the sensational stories that greeted Londoners with their morning tea.

A woman like Finn Parker, living alone and managing her own wealth, would have been unusual. In 1888, a woman without a husband or a father was often viewed with suspicion or considered vulnerable. Respectable women were generally expected to have female companionship in the household to protect their reputation. In the story, Emily Ashworth lives with Finn for this reason, reflecting a common arrangement of the time. Finn moved between the ballrooms of Mayfair and the streets of Whitechapel, observing both.

Montague John Druitt was a real man. He was a barrister and a schoolmaster whose life ended in the

Thames in December 1888. His body was found weeks after the final Ripper murder. Shortly after his death, the police effectively closed the case. Sir Melville Macnaghten later named Druitt as a primary suspect in his private notes, citing "private information" that was never made public.

In these pages, Finn Parker alters this record. She stages a scene to protect the innocent, using existing evidence to create a version of events that history later accepted.

While the "Lightness" and internal discipline of the protagonist come from an older tradition, the world she moves through is entirely Victorian. The Ripper was a man of his time, but Finn Parker moves through time differently.

Investigator's Log

Investigator's Log

Investigator's Log

Investigator's Log

About the Author

Koo Yu is a lifelong reader and writer of crime and mystery fiction. Her love of wuxia tales and stories about heroes who fight for justice inspired her to create Finn Parker, a strong female investigator who moves across time. When she is not writing, she is a marathoner and trail runner who believes every long climb begins with a single step.

Connect with her on X at @kooyuu_writer or via email at kooyu@kooyuwrites.com.

www.ingramcontent.com/pod-product-compliance
Lightning Source LLC
Chambersburg PA
CBHW030240160726
47987CB00020B/473